"Does It Frighten You, Being Here Alone With Me?"

"No," Savannah answered too quickly. "It's just that I, well, I hadn't—" She lifted her gaze to his. It was ridiculous to lie. "Yes."

He took a step back. "I don't want you to ever be afraid of me. You're safe here, Savannah. I promise you that."

He looked at her for a long moment, then said good-night.

Savannah slowly let her breath out and watched him walk away. *Does it frighten you, being here alone with me?*

She wondered what he would say if she told him it wasn't him she was frightened of, but herself.

Dear Reader,

When *Man of the Month* began back in 1989, no one knew it would become the reader favorite it is today. Sure, we thought we were on to a good thing. After all, one of the reasons we read romance is for the great heroes! But the program was a *phenomenal* success, and now, over six years later, we are celebrating our 75th *Man of the Month*—and that's something to be proud of.

The very first *Man of the Month* was *Reluctant Father* by Diana Palmer. So who better to write the 75th *Man of the Month* than this wonderful author? In addition, this terrific story, *That Burke Man,* is also part of her LONG, TALL TEXANS series—so it's doubly special.

There are also five more great Desire books this month: *Accidental Bride* by Jackie Merritt; *One Stubborn Cowboy* by Barbara McMahon; *The Pauper and the Pregnant Princess* by Nancy Martin—which begins her OPPOSITES ATTRACT series; *Bedazzled* by Rita Rainville; and *Texas Heat* by Barbara McCauley— which begins her HEARTS OF STONE series.

This March, Desire is certainly the place to be. Enjoy!

Lucia Macro,
Senior Editor

Please address questions and book requests to:
Silhouette Reader Service
U.S.: 3010 Walden Ave., P.O. Box 1325, Buffalo, NY 14269
Canadian: P.O. Box 609, Fort Erie, Ont. L2A 5X3

BARBARA McCAULEY
TEXAS HEAT

SILHOUETTE *Desire*®

Published by Silhouette Books

America's Publisher of Contemporary Romance

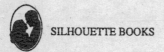

SILHOUETTE BOOKS

ISBN 0-373-05917-5

TEXAS HEAT

Printed in U.S.A.

Books by Barbara McCauley

Silhouette Desire

Woman Tamer #621
Man from Cougar Pass #698
Her Kind of Man #771
Whitehorn's Woman #803
A Man Like Cade #832
Nightfire #875
*Texas Heat #917

*Hearts of Stone

BARBARA McCAULEY

was born and raised in California and has spent a good portion of her life exploring the mountains, beaches and deserts so abundant there. The youngest of five children, she grew up in a small house, and her only chance for a moment alone was to sneak into the backyard with a book and quietly hide away.

With two children of her own now and a busy household, she still finds herself slipping away to enjoy a good novel. A daydreamer and incurable romantic, she says writing has fulfilled her most incredible dream of all—breathing life into the people in her mind and making them real. She has two loud and demanding Amazon parrots named Fred and Barney, and when she can manage the time, she loves to sink her hands into fresh-turned soil and make things grow.

To Barbara A., Stephanie, Terry and Jolie.
Thanks for making this one so much fun.

Prologue

The lawyer's office smelled of money. Old money. Leather armchairs, dark polished woods, plush hunter green carpet. A bronze statue of a horse and rider, silhouetted by the late-afternoon sun, adorned a tall marble stand and stared solemnly out the floor-to-ceiling window overlooking downtown Midland. Silence dominated the room, except for the soft ticktock of the grandfather clock and a woman's muffled whimpering.

Four chairs faced the lawyer's desk. Jake Stone sat in the first, his sister, Jessica, beside him and on the end Myrna Stone, their stepmother. The fourth chair sat conspicuously empty.

Norman Woodard, the lawyer, ran a manicured hand over the silver streak of hair above his left ear, then glanced at the clock. "Mr. Stone, it's already twenty minutes past the hour. We really can't—"

"We wait."

"But—"

Jake lifted his gaze sharply to the man. "I said, we wait."

Woodard's lips tightened, but he said nothing.

Jessica laid a hand over Jake's and he felt the tension slowly ease from his shoulders. His baby sister was no baby anymore, he realized with a note of regret. He could still clearly remember twenty-six years ago, the day his parents had brought her home from the hospital. He'd been only eight at the time, and all he'd seen sticking out of that pink blanket were two huge blue eyes and a crop of shining black hair.

The memory of that day and the happiness in his parents' eyes brought reality crashing back down. They were both gone. His mother twelve years ago, now J.T. Jake closed his fingers tightly around his sister's. At least he still had Jessie. Jessie and ... He stared at the empty chair.

"Mr. Stone," the lawyer tried again, "your brother was given sufficient notice of the day and time of this meeting. I suggest we—"

Tipping back his Stetson, Jake straightened in his chair, knowing that his height had intimidated more than one man. "I just buried my father two days ago, then drove three hours for this meeting. I have two hundred head of cattle to feed, fence to ride and a hay trailer with a flat tire. If I can wait—" he settled back in his chair "—then so can you."

"Mr. Woodard." Jessica leaned forward, and Jake noticed the weary tone in her voice. "These past few days have been difficult, and I'm afraid we're all a little tired. I'm sure my brother will be here any minute."

"Maybe Mr. Woodard is right," Myrna said, worrying the handkerchief in her hands. "After all, it is getting late."

Jake turned to his stepmother. A former Miss Houston, she still looked pretty good at fifty-two. Her blue suit hadn't a wrinkle, nor was one bottle-red hair out of place. Not even a smudge of mascara, though she'd been sniffling and dabbing at her eyes for the past forty-five minutes.

"Maybe *Mr. Woodard* here," Jake said, narrowing his eyes, "doesn't know that flying in from South America isn't exactly a trip to the corner store. And maybe if you hadn't insisted on a funeral that took less time than picking up hamburgers at a drive-through, my brother might have made his father's burial, too."

Myrna's jaw went tight at the sarcasm, but she said nothing, just turned away and stared blankly out the window. For once, Jake thought, the woman knew when to quit.

The clock chimed the half hour.

They waited.

He'd show up. Jake knew he would. It didn't matter that Jared had been gone for three years. It didn't even matter that he hadn't been able to make it to the funeral. All that mattered was that when Jake had finally managed to get a hold of his brother in Venezuela, Jared had said he'd be here. And if it meant camping out in this stuffy lawyer's office until he showed up, then by God, that was what they'd do.

When the three-quarter hour chimed, Mr. Woodard stood. "If you'll excuse me," he said curtly, tugging on the jacket of his precision-cut, tailor-made suit, "I'll go see about having something brought in. Some sandwiches, perhaps, and some drinks—"

"Make mine a rare roast beef" came a deep voice from the back of the room, "and a tall cold beer."

All heads jerked around at the unexpected order. Jared Stone stood in the doorway, his hand on the knob. His denim jacket was worn, but clean, his thick black hair ruffled as if he'd been in a windstorm. A half smile deepened the creases beside his mouth and his eyes—Stone trademark blue—widened with pleasure as he stared at a brother and sister he hadn't seen in three years.

Jessica jumped up from her seat and flew at him, pouncing into his arms as she had when she was a child. Laughing, he lifted her, then spun her around. Jake watched, feeling a strange swelling in his chest as he walked toward his brother. He waited for Jared to put Jessica down before he stuck out his hand.

Jared stared at Jake's hand and his smile slowly faded. The brothers' eyes met, held for one long moment, then, not knowing who moved first and not caring, slapped their arms around each other in a fierce hug.

Jessica circled her arms around both of them and the three of them stood there, sharing the joy of their reunion and the grief that had made it happen.

"Welcome, Mr. Stone," Mr. Woodard interrupted the homecoming. "We're so glad you were able to join us."

"My flight was canceled twice," Jared explained, pulling away from his brother and sister. He noticed his stepmother then and walked over to her. "I'm sorry, Myrna. It must be hard for you."

Myrna's lip quivered as she hugged Jared. "He was fine when I went to town. I came home four hours later and found him in the garage. His heart...it just—" She choked back a sob and wiped at her eyes with her handkerchief.

"Well, now." Mr. Woodard cleared his throat. "Since we're all here, perhaps we can get started."

Nodding, Jake took his seat. Right now, all he wanted was to be alone with his brother and sister, and the sooner they got this over with, the better.

Jessica sat between him and Jared, and Myrna sidled back into her chair. Mr. Woodard, already seated, leaned forward, his hands folded in front of him. "As you may know, your father—" he looked at Jake, then Myrna "—and your husband, came to me six months ago to have a will drawn."

"Why you?" Jake asked. "Cactus Flat is a lot closer to Stone Creek than Midland. Why would he drive all this way just to have a will made?"

"Your father was well-known in Cactus Flat," the lawyer responded. "And because the nature of his requests were somewhat . . . delicate, he thought it best to seek legal counsel elsewhere.''

Delicate, my behind, Jake thought dryly. There hadn't been one thing about J.T. that anyone would have called delicate. ''If you're trying to say that small towns talk, why don't you just spit it out?''

Woodard frowned at the expression. ''There was a concern on your father's part for privacy, Mr. Stone.''

Myrna shifted uncomfortably in her seat. Jessica looked at Jake, then Jared. A heartbeat of silence filled the room like a lead weight.

Jake stared sharply at the lawyer. ''Why don't we just get on with it.''

Nodding, the lawyer straightened his glasses as he lifted the document from its folder.

'''I, Jeremiah Tobias Stone,''' he began, '''of Cactus Flat County, Texas, declare that this is my Will and revoke all prior wills and codicils...''' He droned on, '''...and I name Jake Stone, my eldest son, as Executor of this Will...'''

Eyes narrowed, Myrna turned to Jake, clearly unhappy at J.T.'s choice of an executor. At the mention of her name, she turned back to Woodard.

''' . . . to my spouse, Myrna Stone, I leave my home and its furnishings, plus the surrounding three acres.'''

Myrna's mouth dropped open. Stone Creek was a total of one hundred thousand acres. ''But—'' She started to protest, but the lawyer moved on.

'''...to my son Jake Stone I leave the sixty thousand acres that constitutes Stone Creek ranch, including any existing cattle and assets of that property...'''

Stone Creek Ranch. Jake felt his heart slam against his ribs. He had thought for sure Myrna would get the ranch that he'd run for his father for the past twelve years. Jessica took hold of Jake's hand and squeezed. He knew she understood how important the ranch and Stone Creek were to him.

"But—" Myrna opened her mouth again.

"'...to my son Jared Stone, I leave a parcel of fifteen thousand acres containing a closed-down oil well, plus any and all oil-drilling equipment on the property...'"

Jake looked at his brother. He sat stiff in his chair, his hand tightly clasped on the arm, staring straight ahead. The oil well. Jared's oil well. Three years ago, J.T. had taken it away. Now, in his death, he was giving it back.

Myrna clamped her mouth shut. Her gray eyes glistened with anger, but she said nothing.

"'...and to my daughter, Jessica Stone, I leave fifteen thousand acres that contain the remains of Makeshift, an abandoned town.'"

Stunned, Jessica sat there for a moment, then as she glanced from Jared to Jake, a brilliant smile spread across her face. Jake knew that Jessica had spent half her childhood in the abandoned town. It had been like a giant playhouse for her. What she would do with it now Jake hadn't a clue, but he had no doubt she'd think of something. In fact, based on the look in her blue eyes, the wheels were already turning.

"What about my husband's other assets?" Myrna asked expectantly.

Woodard shook his head. "J.T.'s accountant sent me the past three years of financial statements, Mrs. Stone. It seems that all of his cash and liquid assets were drained to remodel his private residence. There's only a few thousand left, and as stipulated in the will, that money will be equally divided amongst you and his children."

Jake watched Myrna's face turn white at the lawyer's unexpected news. The woman had spent the past ten years building and continuously remodeling a two-story, six-thousand-square-foot monument to herself, and now she had the nerve to sit here and look surprised because there was no more money. If he didn't feel so damn ticked off about it, he might have actually laughed at the irony of it all.

A sour taste rose in Jake's throat. It would hardly affect Myrna, anyway. She not only had money from her first husband, but her own father, Carlton Hewitt *III*, owned half of Houston and was busy trying to buy the rest, as well. What the hell was a few thousand more or less to her, in land or money? Her father had always given her everything she'd wanted. To himself, and to Jared and Jessica, it was the difference between losing Stone Creek or preserving their father's legacy.

And that, above anything else, was what Jake intended to do.

"Well, then," Myrna said crisply as she dropped her handkerchief into her purse and snapped it shut, "if that's all, then—"

"I'm afraid it's not, Mrs. Stone." Everyone turned and looked at the lawyer. He appeared slightly uncomfortable. "There's still one more bequest in the will."

"To the tune of ten thousand acres, I believe," Jake said thoughtfully.

Woodard nodded.

"J.T.'s entire family is sitting in this room," Myrna said sharply. "Who else would my husband leave anything to?"

The lawyer glanced at the document and read, "'To Emma Victoria Roberts Stone.'" He lifted his gaze as he stared at the Stone children. "J.T.'s nine-year-old daughter."

No one moved. It seemed as if no one breathed. Her face rigid, Myrna gripped her black leather purse so tightly it creaked. "Mr. Woodard, J.T. and I were married for eleven years. Surely I'd know if he had . . . that is, if there was an indiscretion of that nature. There must be some mistake."

"I realize what a shock this must be to you all, but your husband did, in fact, father a child, Mrs. Stone. While he was married to you."

"*A sister?*" Jessica whispered, leaning forward in her seat. "We have a sister?"

"Yes, Miss Stone."

Disbelieving, Jessica glanced at both her brothers, then back to the lawyer. "But...how?"

Jared looked at Jessica and raised a brow. "We'll talk later."

Jessica frowned at him. "What I mean is, why didn't we know? How could he not tell us?"

Woodard adjusted his glasses. "It was only recently that your father himself found out. As of this time, I'm afraid our information on the child is extremely limited. We do know that she's nine years old, and we believe she's living in the South somewhere, but that's about it. Your father hired a private investigator to find her, but unfortunately J.T. passed away before the man could locate the mother or the child. However—" the lawyer looked at Jake "—your father has requested in his will that Jake continue the search."

Ignoring Myrna's incredulous look, Jake stared straight ahead. *An affair.* His father had had an affair.

And I have a new kid sister.

"This is ridiculous." Myrna's voice was tight with anger. "Even if there is a child—and I certainly don't believe there is—what difference does it make now? J.T. is gone. There's absolutely no reason to look for her."

Jessica put her hand on Jake's arm. "Of course we'll look for her. Won't we, Jake?"

Jake looked down at his sister. "She's a Stone, isn't she?"

Jessica hugged him, knocking off his Stetson.

"Never a dull moment," Jared said, shaking his head and smiling.

"You sure as hell can say that again," Jake replied, returning his sister's hug. "Welcome home, little brother."

One

The town house was expensive. White wrought iron, beveled windows, shiny brass mailboxes. The taxi slowed, then pulled to a stop in front of a small brick security building nearly engulfed by a creeping vine with pink flowers. The guard behind the polished glass window glanced over his newspaper at the taxi and frowned slightly.

The driver turned to his passenger. "You want me to wait?"

That was a good question, Jake thought. He might be here thirty minutes or thirty seconds. Hell, the woman might not even open the door, in spite of the fact she knew he was coming. It had taken five months after J.T.'s death to track her down, and according to the private investigator, she'd been less than welcoming. Getting her to agree to this meeting had been about as easy as branding a loose steer.

"So how 'bout it?" The cabbie grew impatient. "You want me to wait or not?"

Jake grabbed the small duffel bag on the floor beside him and shook his head. "I'll call."

The guard watched carefully now as Jake paid the fare. It wasn't as if Jake didn't understand the man's concern. This section of Atlanta, Georgia, was much more accustomed to CEOs in tailored suits than a six-foot-four cowboy in a black Stetson and blue jeans.

Hoisting his bag over his shoulder, Jake approached the wary guard. "Afternoon." He touched the brim of his hat. "I'm looking for number 312, Miss Roberts's place."

The man lifted his bushy gray eyebrows and set his paper aside. "And you are?" he asked, pulling out a clipboard.

"Jake Stone."

The guard scanned his daily list of permitted admittances. "Yes, Mr. Stone. Miss Roberts is expecting you. Second sidewalk, turn left. She's the third place in."

He pushed a buzzer and a huge gate opened. Jake stepped inside, then turned to look back when the gate clanked shut behind him. *Damn.* He felt as if he'd just stepped into prison. What the hell kind of place was this that needed high gates and security guards? No place he'd want his kids to grow up. But then, he thought with a frown, since he had no kids and remarriage was definitely not in his plans, where his children were or weren't raised was hardly something to consider.

Shaking his head, Jake followed the guard's directions. Magnolia trees shaded the walkway and bright pink flowers filled the beds. Everywhere he looked was green. A lush deep green that one rarely saw in west Texas. Jake had forgotten there were so many shades of green.

Carolyn, his ex-wife, would have loved this place. The thought made Jake instantly hate it. He wanted out of here, and the sooner, the better.

But he was here for Jessie, Jake reminded himself. He knew that his sister would skin him alive if he didn't come back with some kind of good news. Even Jared had seemed anxious, Jake recalled, remembering the smile in his younger brother's eyes when they'd said goodbye at the airport. It had been a long time since Jared had smiled or seemed enthusiastic about anything, and there was nothing Jake wouldn't do to keep that smile there.

Number 312. Jake stood in front of the door and stared at the shiny brass numbers. A knot began to form in his gut, and though he never would have admitted it, not even to Jessie, a sudden rush of excitement swept through him. Emma Roberts Stone. *J.T.'s child.*

His sister.

"Is he really my brother?" Emma asked for at least the third time in the past half hour. "Is he really?"

Savannah pulled a brush through the child's shining black hair and felt the same twitch in her stomach she'd felt every time her niece asked that question. "We don't know that for sure, Pecan. That's why he's coming over, so we can talk about it."

"It's almost time," Emma said excitedly, twisting her head to glance at the clock. The neat ponytail Savannah had just pulled together disintegrated.

Frowning, Savannah straightened Emma's head and tried again. "Sweetheart, if you don't stop fidgeting, we'll never get your hair done."

The truth, Savannah realized, was that it was her own shaky hands causing the ponytail's demise. He'd be here any minute. Any second.

And she was about to tell the biggest lie of her life.

Forget the ponytail. It didn't matter. But what happened in the next few minutes did matter. More than life itself. Savannah set the brush on the armchair and turned her niece around to face her. Kneeling in front of the child so their eyes met, Savannah touched Emma gently on her cheek.

"Emma, you know I love you more than anything in this world, right?"

Emma nodded, her blue eyes narrowed at the serious tone in her aunt's voice.

"And you know that before your mommy went away she asked me to watch over you and take care of you, too?"

She nodded again.

"That's why you need to do as I asked. You've got to stay in your room and let me talk to this man first. I need to make sure that he is your brother."

Emma drew her brows together. "How will you know?"

Savannah brushed the bangs from the child's face. "You let me worry about that, Pecan."

"Is he going to want me to go live with him?" Emma asked quietly.

The fear in Emma's voice had Savannah pulling her niece into her arms. "Do you think I'd ever let anyone take you away from me?"

The child shook her head.

"Of course I wouldn't. You and I are a team. And I intend to keep it that way." Savannah tightened her hug. "And don't you forget it."

"Okay." Emma hugged her back.

Smiling reassurance she didn't feel, Savannah set her niece away from her and looked into her face. "And stay in the bedroom until I tell you to come out."

"Okay."

The doorbell chimed and they both jumped.

Savannah's stomach tightened. She looked anxiously at the door, then back to Emma. "Go on now, sweetie. I'll let you know when it's all right to come out."

Once her niece had left, Savannah took a deep breath and glanced at the window beside the front door. She saw the outline of a tall man through the partially closed blinds. Maybe he'd go away if she didn't answer. Just give up and go back to Texas. But she knew better. A man didn't spend months tracking someone down and fly all this way just to turn around and leave. He wasn't going to give up and he wasn't going to leave. She had to go through with this. Be done with it now.

He knocked this time. Loudly.

Heart pounding, she moved to the door and opened it.

His black hat was the first thing she noticed about the man, and it struck her how appropriate that seemed. And *tall*. Good God, he towered over her own five-foot-seven frame, and his denim-clad chest and shoulders filled the doorway.

"Miss...Roberts?"

He did not smile as he stared down at her with intense blue eyes. If anything, he was frowning. She watched as he removed his Stetson, revealing hair dark enough to be considered black and a small jagged scar by his right temple.

No doubt this man would try to use his size and menacing looks to intimidate her, Savannah thought with annoyance. He was probably used to women—and men—taking a step back. Resisting the temptation to do just that, she lifted her eyes and met his gaze squarely.

"Mr. Stone." She offered her hand to him and he took it, closing his long fingers over hers. A working man's hand. Large and calloused. She felt strength emanate from him. And determination. Two qualities that could make this meeting difficult.

She pulled her hand from his. "Come in, please."

He dropped his bag on the front porch and stepped inside. His boots sounded heavy on the marble entry. Drawing in a slow, deep breath to steady herself, Savannah closed the door, then gestured to the living room sofa. "Why don't we talk in here?" she said, moving past him.

Confused, Jake stared after the woman. He thought for a moment he had the wrong place, or maybe she was the one who was confused. But she'd looked right at him with eyes as green as a spring meadow and said his name. She couldn't be Angela Roberts, he thought, narrowing his eyes.

Could she?

He watched as she walked away. From her tan high heels to the tips of her honey blond hair, she spelled money. And sex appeal. Definitely sex appeal. Her soft Southern accent flowed over him like warm silk and the faint scent of peaches drifted from her creamy white skin. Her legs were long and slender beneath her knee-length beige skirt, her breasts full and round under a long-sleeved white silk blouse.

Jake could understand how J.T. might have been tempted to take this woman to his bed. Lord knew, *he* certainly was.

She glanced over her shoulder at him and realized he hadn't moved. "Is something wrong?" she asked.

Something *was* wrong, he thought, and followed her into the other room. Very wrong.

She sat on a rose-colored high-back chair and he heard the soft whisper of her stockings as she crossed her legs. He sat on the sofa across from her and sank into the cushions. *Too soft,* he thought almost irritably. And *white.* He almost laughed at the thought of this sofa in his living room. He'd take his firm leather couch over this silly piece of fluff any day.

Glancing around the room, Jake took in the feminine contents: lace curtains, crystal vase on the glass coffee table filled with fragrant pink flowers. Pastel watercolors of garden cottages. A floor-to-ceiling oak bookcase with hardbound novels and floral-framed photographs. Based on the town-house exterior, everything on the inside was exactly as Jake would have imagined. He looked at the woman sitting across from him. Well, *almost* everything.

Savannah didn't like the way Jake Stone was staring at her. Scowling was a more appropriate word. She'd heard that cowboys were the silent type, but this was ridiculous. Other than her name, he hadn't said one word to her. And though she'd already acknowledged that the man had a rugged appeal, she was beginning to wonder if perhaps he'd been kicked by one too many horses.

"Mr. Stone," she said curtly, "could we please dispense with the amenities and get right to the point of your visit? I have an appointment in a little while and I'm afraid I haven't much time."

Jake's frown deepened. He'd nearly drained what was left of his savings to buy a plane ticket, left two hundred head of cattle and spent an entire day traveling just to get here, and *she* hadn't much time? He'd promised Jessie he wouldn't lose his temper no matter what, but this woman was sorely trying his patience.

"I believe Samuels Investigating has already explained in detail why I'm here, Miss Roberts," he said dryly. "But just in case there's some confusion on your part, I'll explain again. I'm here to meet my sister."

Savannah refused to even blink as she stared back at Jake. "And what exactly makes you think Emma is your sister?"

She was cool, aloof even, and except for the tightening of her fingers around the arm of her chair, Jake would have thought her bored. There was something going on under that enticing skin of hers, he realized, and though the idea of exploring that territory appealed to him on a physical level, logic refused to give him more than a passing fantasy.

"Nine years ago you had an affair with my father, J.T. Stone. You disappeared and, according to hospital records uncovered by the P.I., you had a baby seven months later."

She lifted her chin. "That hardly proves your father is responsible."

Jake raised one eyebrow. "Are you saying you were sleeping with two men at the same time?"

Savannah felt her neck, then her cheeks, grow hot. She'd known this was going to be difficult, but she hadn't counted on Jake Stone being so blunt. Damn the man! "Nine years is a long time, Mr. Stone. Whatever happened then has no bearing on now."

The white silk blouse she wore contrasted sharply with the blush on her face, and her reaction to his question surprised Jake. He wouldn't have thought a question of standards would have bothered her. "What did happen?"

It wasn't so much the question he asked as the way he asked it that made Savannah nervous. He was suspicious, she knew it. And she wished to God she could answer him, but the truth was, she didn't know what had happened. Not once in nine years had Angela even hinted at Emma's parentage or the circumstances behind it. With both J.T. and Angela gone, perhaps no one would ever know for sure. "It was just one of those...situations," she said carefully. "There was no reason to burden your father with my...condition."

He was quiet for a moment, as if assessing her and her answer. "Did you love him?" he finally asked.

"I love Emma," she answered quickly, perhaps too quickly. "That's all that matters now. She and I are very happy with the way things are."

She followed his gaze as he looked around the room. "Things appear to be very good, Miss Roberts. Do you have a... roommate?"

Savannah bristled at the implication in his sarcastic tone. She realized an expensive town house like this one would be difficult for most single women to maintain. Lord knew, she never would have been able to afford it on her teacher's salary, but for Angela it had been no problem. The lease was paid up for another four months; then Savannah knew she'd have to move to a smaller place.

"No, Mr. Stone, I don't have a *roommate*. I don't need or want one."

He raised one brow, and when his gaze settled on the hairbrush she'd left lying on the armchair, his eyes narrowed. "And Emma," he said, staring thoughtfully at the brush, "what about her?"

Savannah gritted her teeth at Jake's question, but if answering a few questions would get rid of the man, then she was happy to oblige. "She attends a prestigious private girl's school, has piano lessons every Tuesday and soccer on Saturdays. Other than an occasional argument over eating spinach or picking up her dirty clothes, the two of us get along beautifully."

Jake rested his arms across the back of the couch. His gaze dropped to her left hand. "So you never married."

"No."

"And Emma doesn't know who her father is."

Savannah's jaw tightened. "It wasn't necessary."

"Is that your answer or Emma's?"

Savannah felt as if a band were cinching around her chest, squeezing the breath from her. "I asked you before what you want with us, Mr. Stone. I'll ask you that again."

"And I'll answer you again. I'm here to meet Emma."

"And if I agree, then what?"

"She's my sister. The Stone family never walks away from one of their own."

Panic filled Savannah at Jake's comment. What was he saying? That he wanted to take Emma? She'd never let that happen. *Never.* She'd run so far the Stone family would never find her or Emma.

Shoulders stiff, Savannah stood and faced Jake. "Why you think you have the right to waltz in here and make demands is beyond me, but as far as I'm concerned, this conversation is through. I think you better leave, Mr. Stone."

He didn't budge. Instead, he slowly let his gaze scan her, starting at her legs, hesitating at her breasts, then finally resting on her face. The perusal was long and detailed, and as furious as it made her, Savannah also felt a hot swirl low in her stomach. Clenching her fists, she started to turn toward the front door.

"How old are you, Miss Roberts?"

She went still at his question, then slowly turned back to face him. "Excuse me?"

"I said—" Jake stood "—how old are you?"

Savannah nervously brushed her hair back from her face. "What business is that of yours?"

"I would guess you're around twenty-five or -six."

She said nothing, just stared at him.

"And that would make you about sixteen or seventeen when you had an affair with my father."

Dammit, dammit! There'd been too many years separating her and Angela. Savannah had tried to look older. Conservative clothes and extra makeup. Obviously she'd underestimated Jake Stone.

"I look younger than I am," she said truthfully. She was twenty-seven.

He kept his eyes on her. "What was my father's first name?"

Savannah felt her throat go dry. "J.T., of course."

Impatience twitched at the corner of his mouth. "What was his *first* name?"

How could she possibly know that? Angela had never wanted anyone to know who Emma's father was. If the private investigator hadn't called, Savannah never would have known his name at all. "He didn't tell me."

Jake stared sharply down at her. "You supposedly slept with my father and had his child, but you don't know his first name?"

It was only there for a split second, but Jake saw the fear in the woman's eyes. It was gone as quickly as it appeared, replaced by icy indifference. Lifting her shoulders, she turned stiffly away from him.

"I'll show you out, Mr. Stone."

His hand snaked out, catching her by the elbow and holding her fast. "What the hell kind of a game are you playing?"

She stared down coolly at his hand. "I don't know what you're talking about, but if you don't let go of me and leave right now, I'm going to scream."

He held fast. "Go ahead and scream. Then if I have to bring in a lawyer, we can find out who you really are and why you're lying."

At the mention of a lawyer, she went still. Her frightened gaze darted to his, then, with a long sigh, she closed her eyes. "You don't understand," she said quietly.

"You're damn right I don't understand. But if you think you can put me off while you figure out a way to get your hands on the land, then you're sadly mistaken. There's no way I'm going to stand around and watch while you or anyone else sells off even one foot of Stone Creek."

She looked genuinely confused. "Land? What are you—"

Jake wasn't sure what suddenly caught his attention, a soft cry, or a movement at the hall doorway, but he turned then and saw her. A little girl. Her long hair shone dark as a Texas night, and her eyes, filled now with tears, were as blue as cornflowers.

His heart lurched. He stared at the child and knew without a doubt it was Emma. And he also knew without a doubt that she *was* J.T.'s daughter. The resemblance was uncanny. The little girl was Jessica's clone, right down to the slight cleft in the chin and pert nose. Amazed, he loosened his grip on the woman, but didn't let go. She turned then and saw the child.

"Emma!" She jerked out of his hold and moved across the room to the little girl. "I told you to stay in your room."

"I'm sorry, Aunt Savannah, but I heard somebody yell," Emma said in a tiny shaky voice.

"Oh, sweetheart, I'm sorry if we scared you," Savannah said softly, and took hold of Emma's hand. "We really didn't mean to speak so loud." She turned and sent Jake a piercing look. "Did we, Mr. Stone?"

Jake felt an instant pang of guilt. He was the only one who had raised his voice. Well, hell, he thought, shifting uncomfortably, how was he supposed to know the kid was in the other room?

Jake moved closer to the woman and child, but was careful to keep his distance. "I'm sorry, too, Emma," he said in what he hoped was a reassuring tone. "Your *aunt Savannah* and I were just talking about a few things."

Emma folded herself against Savannah's hip. "About me?"

He nodded. "That's right."

"Are you my brother?" Emma asked, her eyes wide as she stared up at Jake.

Jake looked at Emma, then at the woman the child clung to. "Yes."

Savannah slid a protective hand around Emma's shoulders. "You don't—"

"My name is Jake," he said, "and I have a picture of Jessica, your older sister. Would you like to see it?"

The child's eyes grew even wider. "I have a sister, too?" she asked softly.

"And another brother named Jared," Jake added, pulling a picture from his wallet and handing it to Emma.

"She looks like me!" Emma cried. "Look, Aunt Savannah. My sister, Jessica, looks just like me."

With trembling fingers, Savannah took the picture from her niece, wanting desperately for the child to be wrong. Her heart sank as she stared at the photograph. Though faded from what appeared to be several years in a wallet, there was no mistaking the incredible resemblance between Emma and this woman Jessica.

And no denying the truth.

"Isn't it neat?" Emma looked up at her aunt. "We thought we didn't have any family. Now we have lots!"

Savannah watched Jake's brow furrow at Emma's announcement. Slowly he turned his gaze to meet hers, questioning.

"Yes, Emma, it's...neat." Savannah handed the picture back to Jake. "But they aren't my family, sweetheart, just yours."

"But they have to be yours if they're mine," Emma protested.

"I'll explain later, Pecan." Savannah knelt in front of Emma and pushed the hair away from her cherubic face. "But right now I need to speak to...Jake for a few minutes alone. Okay?"

Emma hesitated, and Jake bent close to her, his face almost level with hers. "I promise I won't leave without saying goodbye."

Jake watched as Emma nodded, then walked down the hall, her eyes downcast. At the sound of the bedroom door closing, Savannah moved away from Jake and stepped toward a sliding glass door that led to a small patio. She stood there, arms folded, and stared out at the potted ferns and azaleas. The door was open a few inches and the lace curtains billowed softly in the cool breeze.

"You want to tell me what's going on?" he asked tersely, moving behind her.

Her shoulders tightened, but she did not turn around. "Emma is my niece," she said quietly. "Angela is...was, my sister."

Was? Jake frowned, letting the impact of Savannah's words settle. He waited silently for her to continue.

"Our parents were killed five years ago in a car accident," she went on. "We have no other family, so Emma always stayed with me when Angela was out of town on business. I loved having her, and because I teach at St. Mary's Academy here in Atlanta where Emma is in the fourth grade, it was also convenient."

Savannah's hand reached out to smooth the lace curtain, and as she did so, the breeze carried the sound of tinkling wind chimes from the patio outside.

"Go on," he encouraged when she hesitated.

She drew in a deep breath, then slowly let it out. "Angela had just received an award for her design of a contemporary art museum in Florida. She'd been gone four days and was anxious to get home. When her flight was canceled, she chartered a private plane to fly her home."

Savannah turned, and though she looked directly at Jake, he realized she didn't really see him. "Her birthday was last week. She would have been forty-three."

Jake felt his gut tighten. Children needed a mother. And a father. At nine years old, Emma had neither. "What do you know about my father and your sister?"

Savannah shook her head. "Nothing. Angela was sixteen years older than me, more like a mother than a sister. I was only eighteen when she came back from a job in Texas. She kept that part of her life completely private, and all I knew was that she'd fallen in love with an older, married man. I'd always assumed he'd turned his back on her when he found out she was pregnant."

"My father wouldn't have done that," Jake said coldly.

"Did you know your father was having an affair?"

"Of course not."

"Then how do you know what else he did or didn't do?"

Jake's face was etched in granite, and his eyes narrowed as he stepped closer. "I know that no member of the Stone family would ever walk away from one of their own."

"Emma is not 'your own,'" she said fiercely. "She is Emma Victoria Roberts, and she's mine. I laughed in the delivery room when she was born, applauded her on the soccer field when she got her first goal and cried with her when her mother died. For nine years she's done fine without you and will continue to do so for ninety more."

She faced him like a lioness defending her young, her green eyes flashing a challenge and her chin lifted defiantly. The breeze tugged at the ends of her shoulder-length blond hair, and he couldn't help but notice the graceful sweep of her slender fingers as she absently brushed the strands back.

He moved closer to her, and the scent of magnolias drifted in from the open door. He'd heard the term "steel magnolia" before, but he'd never been face-to-face with it. He felt a tug of desire as he stared at the woman, then reminded himself she'd lied to him. There were few things he tolerated less than lying. Very few things. "Why did you pretend to be Angela?" he asked tightly.

Sighing, she closed her eyes, then opened them again. "Emma is all I have. Surely you can understand that I would do anything to protect her."

Jake frowned. "You thought you had to protect her from her own brother?"

"Half brother," she corrected him.

His jaw tightened. "Family is family. All I want, and Jessica and Jared, as well, is an opportunity to get to know Emma, and for her to know us."

The fear was back again, Jake noticed. Her green eyes darkened with it momentarily before she quickly wrestled it down. He couldn't help but give her credit for her control.

"I suppose," she said, and that enticing accent of hers turned icy. "If you call first, we might be able to make arrangements for visits."

The idea of making arrangements grated on Jake's already shredded patience almost as much as Savannah's cool formality. Tipping his hat back, he let out a heavy sigh. "Well, now, ma'am—" he forced a heavy Texas drawl "—that's right nice of you, but that's not exactly what I had in mind."

"Oh?" She lifted one delicate eyebrow. "And what exactly did you have in mind?"

"What I have in mind—" his gaze locked with hers and his voice dropped dangerously low as he stepped closer "—is for my little sister to come home with me."

Two

It was her worst nightmare come true. The very thing she'd dreaded since the day she'd received the phone call from the private investigator. Savannah felt her skin go cold and her heart stop for one terrifying split second.

Nobody was taking Emma away from her. *Nobody*.

She stared at Jake, letting the shock wave travel through her, and felt relief at the anger that followed in its wake. She knew better than to show weakness to a man like Jake Stone. Lifting her chin, she faced him and locked his intense gaze with her own. "I don't know you from Adam, Mr. Stone. I wouldn't let you take my niece around the block, let alone to Texas. Emma is in my charge and she stays with me."

Jake shrugged. "I don't have a problem with that. There's plenty of room for both of you."

Go to Texas? He couldn't be serious. He *couldn't*. But he was, Savannah realized. Dead serious. "That's ridiculous."

He walked to her, stopping so close she felt the heat of his body and smelled the pure masculine scent that radiated from him. She desperately wanted to step away, but refused to give in to his obvious attempt at intimidation.

"Why?" he asked.

Why? There were at least a dozen logical reasons she could easily throw at him—two dozen—but she was having a difficult time thinking with him so close. "Because... because we can't, that's why."

He raised one eyebrow. "Is school out for you and Emma?"

"We finished three days ago, but—"

"Fine. Then you can get someone to watch this place for you for a couple of months."

"A couple of months!" Savannah's mouth dropped open. "That's out of the question."

"All right, then," Jake conceded. "A month."

How had this gotten so out of hand? A month with this man to— *Where* was it he lived? Stone Creek? She'd be crazy to even consider it. Shaking her head, Savannah turned away and stared out the glass door. "I'm sorry, but it's just not possible."

"I'll petition the courts if necessary," he said dryly. "As Emma's brother, I have a right, legally and morally, to visitation. You can come with her or not. Either way, it's your choice."

Cold fear gripped Savannah. He was making it perfectly clear that if she forced him to petition the court and he won, she would be excluded from the visit. If she agreed to the visit, then she could come. She turned stiffly. "I believe that's blackmail, Mr. Stone. You'll win the game at any cost, won't you?"

His mouth tightened at her accusation. "I'm not looking to win the game, Miss Roberts. I'm only asking that you deal me—and my sister and brother—a fair hand."

"Fair?" She whirled away, then turned back around, her hands on her hips. "I never heard of Stone Creek or your family until two weeks ago. And now, suddenly, here you are, demanding that I let Emma visit you, and you have the nerve to talk to me about fair? For all I know, you just got out of prison."

"You'll have to trust me on that one."

She nearly laughed at the absurdity of his comment. "Mister, right now I wouldn't trust you with an old pair of socks, let alone my niece. Emma is all I have, and I'm all she has. If the situation were reversed, what would you do?"

He stared at her for a long moment, his gaze hard and cold. Then unexpectedly he looked away, removing his hat and running a work-roughened hand through his hair. "Look, Miss Roberts...Savannah," he said more softly, "I realize how difficult this must be for you. And you're right, if the situation were reversed, I'd do exactly the same." He sighed heavily. "But answer me this—what plans have you made for Emma if anything happens to you?"

An image of her hand locked with Emma's as they stood beside Angela's coffin intruded into Savannah's mind. Who would hold her niece's hand if tragedy struck again? She nearly shivered at the thought. "Nothing is going to happen to me."

"But if something does, where will Emma go? You already said you have no family. But Emma does. She has me and Jessica and Jared. Give us a chance. At least come and meet us, and you'll know we'll always be there for her if she needs us."

The reality of Jake's words swept through Savannah with the chill of an arctic wind. He was right. No one knew what tomorrow might bring, and if anything did happen to her, at least Emma wouldn't be with strangers, with people who didn't care about her.

She'd be with family.

Savannah realized that, regardless of whether she wanted to go or not, she *needed* to. She needed the peace of mind that, if it became necessary, the Stone family would care for Emma as their own. That they would love her and protect her.

Forcing herself not to tremble, Savannah faced Jake. "Your wife won't mind?"

Jake frowned. "It's just me and Jared and Jessica."

Savannah drew in a deep shaky breath, then slowly released it. "One month." She leveled her gaze on his. "But if I think, even for a second, that you or your family might hurt Emma, then we'll be gone so quick your head'll spin faster than one of your Texas tornadoes." *And you'll never find us again.*

Relief softened the corners of Jake's eyes, and he smiled for the first time, extending his hand. "I'll send the tickets right away."

"I'll make the arrangements myself, thank you."

Hesitantly she took his hand. His warm, rough fingers closed over hers and something passed between them. Something that made Savannah catch her breath and Jake's eyes sharpen. It was softer than a whisper and lighter than the brush of a feather.

And *it,* whatever it was, packed the punch of a twenty-ton press.

She pulled her hand abruptly away and folded her arms, praying she wasn't making the biggest mistake of her life.

Savannah had no trouble finding Jake when she and Emma got off the plane six days later. After all, spotting a six-foot-four cowboy wearing a black hat in the middle of a crowded airport was hardly a difficult task.

But what *was* difficult for her was the way her heart slammed against her ribs and her pulse shifted into double time at the sight of him.

He stood off to the side, leaning casually against a ticket counter, his face shielded by the brim of his hat. His white workshirt was clean and pressed, and he'd hooked his thumbs into the front loops of his jeans. A silver buckle gleamed at his narrow waist, and though she tried, it was impossible to stop her gaze from drifting downward, over his lean hips to the masculine bulge at the juncture of his long legs. She tore her gaze quickly away, but not before the heat of a blush warmed her cheeks.

"Aunt Savannah!" Emma tugged on her hand and pointed. "There's Jake!"

He caught sight of them and straightened, then reached down to pick up a shopping bag at his feet.

"Jake!" Emma called to him and waved. "Here we are!"

Emma had been a bundle of energy and excitement all week. She'd asked endless questions about the Stone family that Savannah couldn't answer and had packed and re-packed her bags countless times. Savannah, on the other hand, had been a bundle of nerves. As she'd prepared her own suitcases, the temptation to take her niece and run had been overwhelming.

But she hadn't, of course. And now, as Jake Stone strolled determinedly toward her and Emma, Savannah once again wished she had.

He stopped in front of them, his gaze intense as it slid slowly over Savannah. She'd tried to convince herself that she'd imagined that feeling she'd had the last time he'd looked at her this way, but she hadn't. *It* was there again between them. Unspoken, but every bit as powerful as before, and Savannah nearly shivered with the force of it. There was a taut moment of silence before he looked over at Emma and reached into the bag he carried.

"I thought you might like this," he said to Emma, and pulled out a fluffy white stuffed animal.

"A kitty! Thanks, Jake." Emma hugged the present to her. "Did you bring anything for Savannah?"

"Not this time," he said, and when he turned his gaze back to Savannah the predatory look that flashed through his blue eyes made her pulse skip. "Maybe next time."

"There's nothing I need, thank you," Savannah said, meeting Jake's dark gaze, though her throat was so dry she hardly knew how she got the words out. "You just concentrate on Emma."

Jake knew that Savannah was right, of course. He'd brought his sister to Stone Creek for a family gathering, not to get her beautiful aunt into his bed. But when he'd looked at her after she'd stepped off the plane, that had been his first thought. That pink slip of a dress she was wearing might be cool for her, but it had him so hot it was damn near embarrassing. What red-blooded male wouldn't look at those long smooth legs and imagine them wrapped around his waist?

Jake nearly sighed aloud at the thought. With all the problems he'd been having since he'd had to fire his only ranch hand a month ago, there'd been no time to even consider female companionship, let alone do anything about it. To Jake, lust and sex were as natural a part of life as breathing. But since his ex-wife, he'd taught himself to control those urges with women. Savannah Roberts would be no different, he told himself.

Still, he'd seen the interest flare in her green eyes, too, whether she was willing to admit it or not. Maybe, just maybe, if the time and place were right and the lady was willing...

The midmorning air was cool, so they drove with the windows down. Jake had borrowed Jessica's station wagon, and the car, though certainly not new, was comfortable and clean, two things Jake's truck was not. Emma was stretched out in the back seat, firing questions at Jake about his ranch and Jared and Jessica and what kind of animals he had. He patiently answered them all, until finally, as the drive wore on, she fell asleep.

Savannah looked behind her at the exhausted child and smiled. "She's been up since five. I'm surprised she lasted this long."

"You look tired yourself." Jake adjusted the rearview mirror. "Why don't you go ahead and take a nap? It's still another two hours to the ranch."

"Two hours?" Savannah looked at the expanse of land in front of her. As far as the eye could see were mesquite and sagebrush, cacti with yellow blooms and tall porcupine-looking plants with white flowering spikes. Low-lying mountains hovered at the horizon, and dark clouds prowled the outer ridges. There were no signs of people, no buildings. Just land, and more land.

"Isolated" was the word that came to mind. She'd been nervous about coming here, but never actually afraid. Until now. "You didn't mention your place was so far away from the airport."

From people.

The radio was more static than music. Jake fiddled with the dial for a moment, then shut it off. "Does that bother you, being far away?"

"Well, no, of course not, it's just that, well, I might need some things. A month is a long time."

"Cactus Flat is about forty-five minutes from the ranch. You can get most anything you need there, except for fast food or sushi," he added.

With a place that sounded as warm and welcoming as Cactus Flat, Savannah could hardly wait. "No fast food?" She opened her eyes wide in feigned disbelief. "I had no idea we'd be roughing it like this."

Her sarcasm brought a frown to his face. "People from the city think life out here is a stroll in the park, Savannah. Pretty little horses and cute little cows." His frown deepened. "Ranching is hard, dangerous work. Long hours, no medical pay, no sick leave."

He was angry, Savannah realized. His words were bitter, and she almost felt as if he was intentionally painting a bleak picture for her. That hardly made sense, since he'd pushed so hard to get her and Emma out here.

"So why do you do it if you feel that way?" she asked.

His frown softened and he stared out the windshield, his gaze briefly following the dive of a hawk overhead. "I could no more explain it than you could ever understand it. It's just what I do, that's all."

Savannah pressed her lips tightly together. "I might understand more than you think, Jake. Why don't you get to know me a little better before you pass judgment on me?"

He turned to her then and a smile lifted one corner of his mouth. His deep blue eyes darkened and narrowed with a look of intense masculine interest. She nearly shivered at the response that rose unwillingly in her.

"I'll do that," he said huskily.

Heat shimmered over her skin and she looked quickly away before he could see the blush she knew was working its way up her cheeks. It was suddenly stifling in the car, but she refused to ask him to turn on the air. She'd show Jake Stone she was tough as any Texas rancher.

"Savannah?"

She heard someone calling her name, but just couldn't quite pull herself from the leaden mist wrapped around her. She turned her head slightly, but a soft "Hmm?" was all she could manage.

The voice came again, "Savannah."

It was a nice voice, she decided. Deep, with a rough, gravelly texture that sent warm tingles over her skin. It sounded just like—

Jake!

She opened her eyes then, startled to realize she'd fallen asleep. He was leaning close to her, so close she felt the warmth of his breath on her cheek.

"Wake up, sleepyhead," he whispered. "We're here."

His words, along with the intimate tone of his voice, made Savannah's pulse race. Embarrassed, she sat upright and leaned away from him. "I—I'm sorry. I must have been more tired than I realized."

"Emma, too," he said quietly, pointing to the back seat. "She's been out the whole time."

Savannah glanced at her sleeping niece. Though still buckled in, she lay sprawled across the seat, her ponytail gone and in its place a tousled mass of shining black hair.

Jake shut off the engine. The sudden stillness had Emma sitting up. Her eyes shot open and she looked out the car window. "Are we here? Is that your house?"

Savannah glanced at the one-story rambling home. It was a practical house of sturdy brick and rock. No flowers, no frills. Built rugged to survive the elements. Like the man himself, she thought.

Distant windmills dotted the land beyond the house, and a huge barn several hundred yards away caught Emma's attention.

"Do you have horses in there?" Emma asked excitedly. "Can I see them?"

"A little later." Jake reached over and unbuckled Emma's seat belt. "Right now there're some people who've been waiting to meet you."

While Jake got the luggage, Savannah quickly pulled a brush through Emma's tangled hair, then her own. Her hand shook slightly as she hurriedly applied lipstick. Jared and Jessica were waiting inside. And while Savannah knew that they certainly would like Emma, she couldn't help but wonder what they would think of her. Would they consider her an outsider? An intruder?

Inside the house there were pink and white balloons and streamers everywhere. They seemed strongly out of place in the masculine interior of dark wood and leather furniture.

Jake, with one bag under each arm and another in each hand, kicked the door shut behind him.

A man stood just inside the door, his hands in the back pockets of his faded jeans. He was nearly as tall as Jake, with the same muscular build, but his hair was a shade lighter, and his blue eyes, though smiling, held a strange sadness. The kind of sadness a woman could easily find herself drawn to, Savannah thought.

A young woman wearing a sleeveless white denim shirt and black jeans came out of the kitchen drying her hands on a towel. *Jessica.* The minute Savannah saw her she felt her breath catch. She was beautiful. And if the resemblance between Emma and Jessica's photograph had been strong, in real life it was amazing.

Jessica tossed the towel aside and moved in front of Emma. There was silence for a moment as Jessica and Jared looked at Emma, then Jessica bent down and held out her hand. "Hello, Emma."

Still clutching the stuffed animal Jake had given her, Emma suddenly turned shy and leaned close to Savannah. "It's all right, Pecan." Savannah nudged her niece. "Say hello to your sister."

Emma took a cautious step forward. "Are you really my sister?"

Jessica nodded.

Hesitantly Emma took Jessica's hand. "Are you having a party?" she asked, looking around the room.

Jessica smiled. "It's a welcome party for you."

"For me?" Emma's eyes widened. "Thank you!"

As Jake watched Emma move into Jessica's arms and give her a hug, he felt his throat tighten. He knew that if his mother hadn't nearly died giving birth to Jessica there would have been a dozen more Stone children. But Jake's father had loved his wife too much to chance losing her and so had made sure no more children were conceived. Something told Jake that if his mother were alive, she would have welcomed this child. His stepmother, on the other hand, was an entirely different matter.

When Emma gave Jared a hug, too, Jake cleared his throat loudly and set the bags down. "Hey, what about me? I brought you here, didn't I?"

Emma ran to Jake and nearly jumped into his arms. Savannah stood by, feeling completely out of place as she watched the family unite. It seemed so natural, she thought, watching Emma wrap her arms around Jake's neck. As if they'd known each other forever.

Jessica, her eyes glistening with tears, stepped forward and took hold of Savannah's hands. "How can we ever thank you?"

Savannah shook her head. "It's not necessary." And when she glanced at Jake and saw him smiling down at Emma, she knew in that second she'd done the right thing by coming. She knew that no matter what happened to her, Emma would always be loved and cared for.

And as comforting as that realization was, a cold shiver of fear went through Savannah. For she knew in her heart that the love that would protect Emma might also take her away.

Jessica, still holding on to Savannah, took Emma's hand, as well, and pulled them both toward the kitchen. "You two must be starving. I have a pizza almost ready to come out of the oven, cold cuts and potato salad and beans and franks. Oh, and chocolate cake for dessert."

"So what's Jake going to eat?" Jared teased.

"His boots if he doesn't hurry up," Jessica called back.

Jake tossed his hat onto a hook in the entry and made his way to the kitchen. "Couldn't tell the difference between my boots and that steak Jared made last week. What was in that marinade, Bro? Boot wax?"

The banter continued through lunch. Emma giggled at the silliness and even Savannah felt herself relaxing. The kitchen was large and sunny, but once again, there was no woman's touch here, she noted. No curtains, no basket of dried flowers or wooden cows hanging on the wall. Simple and utilitarian in appearance, but complete with what appeared to be most of the necessary modern appliances.

Savannah found herself wondering why Jake hadn't married and why this kitchen wasn't filled with his own children. Had it become comfortable living with Jessica and Jared, or was he just too busy to look for a wife?

As if this man would have to look far, she told herself, glancing sideways at him. If word got out he was looking for a wife, the three-hour drive to Midland would be bumper to bumper with eager females.

"Would you like a roll?"

Startled from her thoughts, Savannah realized Jake was talking to her. "Excuse me?"

"A roll." He offered her a basket of bread. "You want one?"

Jake had no idea what had brought the sudden flush to Savannah's cheeks, but he couldn't stop his own thought, which was wondering if her face flushed with passion as easily as it did with embarrassment. He had a swift and fervent desire to find out, and if Jessica hadn't announced it was time for everyone to have cake, he might have let his imagination wander a bit.

Emma giggled when Jared got chocolate frosting on his chin and the sound flowed through Jake like warm honey. Emma had brought something into his house he hadn't realized he'd missed. People and laughter. She hadn't been here two hours and already he was wondering how he could let her leave. A month was too short.

But that was something he'd deal with later. He looked at Savannah, watching as she licked a spot of frosting from her upper lip. The innocent, but sensuous gesture had his groin tightening painfully, and he began to realize that a month might, in fact, be a very long time.

"Hello? Anybody home?"

Jake went still at the sound of the voice, as did everyone else in the kitchen. Jake frowned at Jessica, then Jared, but they both shook their heads.

He counted to three, struggling to control his temper, furious that this special party was being interrupted.

Myrna had just walked in his front door.

Three

The sudden tension in the room closed around Savannah like a fist. Instinctively she put her arm around Emma, who was busy spearing a bite of cake, oblivious to any change in the atmosphere.

The voice came again. "Jake?"

He scowled. Jared shook his head and quickly covered Jessica's mouth. Jessica pushed Jared's hand away. "In here," she called out, and punched Jared's arm.

"There you are." An older redheaded woman in a green crepe suit appeared at the doorway. She slipped her sunglasses off. "Are you having a party?"

Jake stood and faced the woman. "I thought you were in Houston visiting your father this week, Myrna."

With a sigh, the woman swept into the room, her gaze directed downward as she tucked the sunglasses into her clutch purse. Her heels clicked loudly on Jake's tile floor. "I was, but he was in business meetings night and day, so I decided to come home early. You'd think at seventy-three he could pass up at least one land deal and spend a little time with his only daughter."

"You usually call me for a ride from the airport," Jessica said.

"Since that little accident I had, Daddy insisted I hire a driver. So when William came by looking for employment, I took him on."

"William?" Jake stared at his stepmother. "You mean Billy who used to work for me?"

"Yes, that's him." She snapped her purse shut and straightened her suit jacket.

Jake nearly choked. "Myrna, I fired the man because he has a drinking problem."

"Nonsense. William is as dry as—" She stopped, her brow lifting in question as her gaze rested on Savannah. "Oh. You have company."

The momentary silence was deafening. Who was this woman? Savannah wondered. And why was everyone acting so strangely? She glanced at Jake, and the tight expression on his face had her holding her breath.

"Myrna Stone," he finally said, "Savannah Roberts."

Myrna Stone. Savannah had heard the name, but where? Myrna Stone...Myrna Stone... Her breath caught as the realization hit her full force.

J.T.'s wife.

Before she came here, Savannah had realized that she and this woman might meet. But she certainly hadn't expected it the first day. Savannah's fingers stiffened on her niece's back. *Emma.* Dear Lord, what about Emma?

"A pleasure." Myrna extended her hand, then glanced down at Emma. "And this must be your daugh—"

Myrna stopped short, her smile frozen on her face. She stared at Emma, then Jessica, recognizing the resemblance.

Savannah stood slowly and faced the woman. "Emma is my niece, Mrs. Stone. Angela Roberts—Emma's mother— was my sister."

A lifetime passed through the heartbeat of silence.

Emma took hold of Savannah's hand. "Did she know my daddy, too, Aunt Savannah?"

"Yes, sweetheart, she did," Savannah answered, keeping her gaze on the woman.

Myrna's face had paled at Emma's question, and as she stared at the child, Savannah felt a wave of sympathy for the woman. Of course she'd be in shock at the realization she was staring at the child her husband had fathered as the result of an extramarital affair. Anger surged through Savannah. Anger at Jake. He should have prepared her for the possibility that the woman might drop by, just as he should have prepared his stepmother. But he hadn't.

Eyes wide, Myrna continued to stare at Emma. "You mean, this is . . . she's my husband's—"

Jessica stood quickly. "Emma, why don't we go wash some of that chocolate off your face? When we're done, if it's okay with your aunt, we can go out to the barn and feed Jake's new calf."

"Is it okay, Aunt Savannah? Can I?" Emma asked eagerly.

"Of course you can, sweetie." Savannah forced herself to smile at her niece. "I'll join you in a few minutes."

Emma chattered all the way down the hall. When they were out of earshot, Myrna turned to Jake. "Would you please explain to me what's going on?"

Jake had known he'd have to deal with his stepmother sooner or later, he'd just hoped it would be later. *Dammit.* Why couldn't she have stayed in Houston like she was supposed to? "Emma is J.T.'s daughter, Myrna. Her mother died eight months ago and Emma lives with Savannah now. I've invited them to stay here for a while."

"Stay here?" Myrna looked genuinely confused. "You've invited my husband's illegitimate child to stay *here?*"

Jake saw the indignant lift of Savannah's chin and stiffness in her shoulders. It was all he could do not to throttle his stepmother. "Emma is my sister, Myrna—"

"Our sister," Jared added sharply, rising from his seat.

Jake stood a step closer to Myrna. "*Our* sister," he repeated. "And I might remind you that she has Stone blood in her veins."

Distress deepened the lines around Myrna's eyes. "Jake, surely you can understand my reaction. It's not easy to have J.T.'s—" she hesitated, as if searching for another word "—indiscretion waved under my nose like this."

"*Emma,*" Jake said through clenched teeth. "Her name is Emma. You refer to her as anything other than her given name, and so help me, I'll personally show you the door."

Myrna clutched a hand to her throat, then looked at Savannah. "Miss Roberts, forgive me. I meant no offense. It's just that this has all come as a shock to me. I had no idea that you and . . . Emma were staying here."

"I understand your surprise, Mrs. Stone." Savannah shot Jake a heated look. "But you needn't worry yourself about it. We'll be leaving tomorrow."

Jake's head turned sharply. "What are you talking about?"

Savannah gathered up a few dirty dishes. "There's an afternoon flight tomorrow. I'm sure we'll be able to catch it." Ignoring the dark look on Jake's face, she moved around him and deposited the dishes in the sink. "Now, if you'll excuse me, I think I'll join my niece in the barn."

She'd barely made it off the front porch before Jake's hand took hold of her arm and pulled her around to face him.

"What the hell do you think you're doing?" he snapped.

"I'm going to the barn."

"You know what I mean. We had an agreement."

"That's right, we did." Savannah put her hands on her hips and leaned forward. "I told you that if you or anyone in your family hurt Emma, we'd be gone before you could blink."

"Myrna was supposed to be in Houston. I had no idea she'd turn up here today."

"I'm not talking about Myrna. I'm talking about you. You never considered what might happen or how Emma would feel if your stepmother showed up. You only thought about what you wanted."

His eyes narrowed as he stared down at her. "Okay. I messed up."

"You got that right, mister." The air was dry outside and a hot wind whipped her hair in front of her face, but she ignored it. She leaned even closer to Jake and lifted her face to his. "When Angela died I made a vow that nothing was ever going to hurt Emma again. Nothing—" she pressed a finger to Jake's chest "—and no one."

Frustration had Jake wrapping his hand tightly around Savannah's. "Dammit, Savannah, I care about Emma. We all do. I admit I made a mistake and I can't promise I won't make more. But I can promise I'll try my damnedest." He loosened his hold on her and his voice softened. "Give me a chance."

Could she take that kind of risk when it came to Emma? Savannah asked herself as she stared into Jake's eyes. She'd sworn that her niece would never feel pain again, but in reality, she knew that some pain was inevitable. There were times when people would be cruel. And a loving supportive family would be the only safe haven. Jake and Jared and Jessica had already proved they could supply that haven by the way they'd banded together to handle their stepmother. In her heart she knew it would be wrong to take Emma away so soon.

But Savannah's heart was telling her something else. Something she did not want to listen to. Something was happening here between her and Jake. Something that would only complicate matters. She stared at Jake's hand still covering her own and suddenly realized how close she was standing to him. Her fingers rested against his rock-hard chest and she felt the steady beat of his heart.

"She's just a little girl, Jake," Savannah said quietly. "Angela and I have always done our best to shelter her. She doesn't understand how cruel some people can be."

He stroked the soft skin of her palm, and it was impossible for Savannah to stop the shiver that coursed up her arm and through her body.

"I'll horse-drag anyone who even looks at her cross-eyed, myself included," he said. "You can ride the horse."

"I suppose Emma would be upset if we left so soon," she murmured, and found that her throat was as dry as the Texas dust swirling around her feet. She felt the heat of his skin radiate through his cotton shirt.

"So would I."

Without her realizing when, he'd pulled her against him. They stood there at the base of the porch, their bodies touching, his hand stroking hers. It seemed to Savannah that her bones were softening and she felt a yearning she'd never experienced before. She leaned against Jake, felt the heat of the sun on her back and his muscled body pressed against her thighs and breasts. Desire spilled through her, making her ache to be closer, to—

"Aunt Savannah!"

Savannah jerked her hand away from Jake's at the sound of Emma's call. Her niece was running back from the barn with Jessica several feet behind.

"Aunt Savannah! Come see the baby cow! My sister, Jessica, says I can feed it a bottle."

Savannah hadn't seen that big a smile on Emma's face since before Angela had died. It was worth all the gold in the world to Savannah. She waved to her niece with a shaky hand. "I'll be right there, Pecan."

She looked back at Jake and nodded slowly. "Okay, Mr. Stone, I'll give you another chance." She turned to follow

Emma, wondering how she could walk on knees that felt like warm rubber.

Jake watched Savannah walk away and breathed a heavy sigh of relief. The first day and already he'd nearly blown it. Myrna hadn't been expected until next week. He'd planned on telling Savannah about his stepmother then. How the hell could he have known that she'd show up today of all days?

"Jake?"

He turned. Billy stood behind him, his hat in his hand, his gaze cast downward. Myrna's white luxury sedan was parked a few feet away.

"Hello, Billy."

"I know you're probably still sore at me, but I just wanna say I'm sorry for any trouble I caused ya. I oughtn't not been drinking like that on your time."

Jake frowned at the man. He looked as if he'd tied one on the night before. Jake sighed inwardly. Only his stepmother would hire a drunk to drive for her. "You go to any AA meetings yet?"

"One."

"Get yourself straightened out, then come see me in the fall."

"Yes, sir."

Jake turned and went back into the house. Billy was Myrna's problem. And right now, he and his stepmother were going to have to get a few things straight about Savannah and Emma.

Because now that he had them here, he intended to make sure they stayed.

The hot water did wonders for Savannah's frazzled nerves. Sighing, she stood under the pounding shower head, letting the needlelike spray relax her tense shoulders. To say that her first day at Stone Creek had been long was the understatement of the century, but after Myrna had left, everyone, including herself, had calmed down and enjoyed the rest of the day.

Emma was already asleep. Savannah had tucked her in only minutes ago and the child's eyes had closed immediately, a smile on her angelic face. Savannah's own lips curved as she recalled the excitement on Emma's face as she'd bottle-fed the calf that afternoon. The nine-year-old had never even seen a cow before, let alone fed one.

Eyes closed, Savannah leaned her head back and rinsed her hair. Shampoo and water sluiced over her flushed skin. She felt herself slowly relax, and she let her mind wander, assessing her first day at Stone Creek and the man who had brought her here.

Jake Stone. Hardworking rancher, as devoted to his family's land as he was to the family itself. Yet he had no family of his own. No wife. No children. He seemed to hold part of himself back, watching more than participating.

And he'd watched her, too, she realized. He'd watched her with the same intensity that a wild animal might observe its prey. Calculating and bold. Determined. She shivered despite the heat of the pulsing water. She'd felt, more than seen, the heat of his stare. Felt it on some primal level she didn't understand and had never experienced before with any man. It frightened her.

It excited her.

Reluctantly Savannah shut off the water and stepped out of the shower. Her first day here and already she'd made a fool of herself. She'd practically melted in the man's arms this afternoon. She groaned softly, remembering how she'd leaned into him when he'd held her hand.

She refused to give in to any attraction she might feel for Jake. The feeling would pass, she told herself, though she really hadn't much experience to base that belief on. She'd never met, or reacted to, any man like Jake before. She was completely out of her element. It was much easier, and much more comfortable, to date men who didn't intimidate the hell out of her.

Savannah couldn't imagine that there would be anything easy or comfortable when it came to Jake. He'd barely touched her this afternoon, and yet she could still feel the coarse texture of his thumb on her palm and the electricity that touch had sent through her. She rubbed the towel roughly over her skin and her hair, as if she might scour the feeling away, but it only intensified.

Swearing under her breath, she yanked a comb through her tangled hair and slipped on her nightgown and robe. Thank goodness Jessica was here as a buffer, she thought. A month would go by quickly and she and Emma would leave, no worse for wear.

She felt better already as she stepped out of the bathroom and headed for the guest bedroom beside Emma's. Family pictures lined the hallway, and Savannah paused, quickly scanning the photos—Jake as a young boy, sitting on a horse as he waved a cowboy hat; Jessica in pigtails with one tooth missing; Jared and another boy the same age, riding bicycles, though she couldn't see the second boy's face.

An old wedding picture caught her attention and she moved closer to that one, trying to read a date in the corner.

"My parents' wedding portrait."

Savannah jumped at the sound of Jake's voice so close to her ear. She hadn't heard him come up behind her. "They...look very happy."

"They were." He stepped closer and stared at the picture, looking at it as if he hadn't seen it for a long time. "He was never the same after she died."

"My parents died together," she said quietly. "I'd never really thought about it, but I realize now it would have been harder for the survivor if only one had died."

"I kept him company with an occasional bottle for a while," Jake admitted. "But he needed a different kind of company."

"Myrna?" Savannah asked.

He nodded and it seemed as if he was looking through the picture, instead of at it. "Men make mistakes when they're lonely."

Savannah detected a note of bitterness in Jake's voice, and something told her he wasn't just talking about his father. She started to turn then, preparing to say good-night, when another picture caught her eye. It was a photograph of a sprawling white two-story mansion. A circular driveway led to a set of double doors. Barely discernible, a man stood in the open doorway, his muscular arms folded as he smiled for the camera. Savannah froze. She'd seen this picture before. She knew this house.

Eyes wide, she turned to Jake. "Where did you get this picture?"

"That's the house my father built for Myrna. Stone Manor, she calls it." He frowned at Savannah. "Is something wrong?"

She turned back and stared at the photo. "This house— my sister designed it. She has—had—this picture, along with the blueprints, in her portfolio."

Silence echoed in the hallway. They were both looking at not only a piece of the past, but of the puzzle.

"That explains how they met," Jake said at last, then gave a dry laugh.

Savannah glanced over her shoulder. "What?"

"Myrna hired the architectural firm and asked for the best. Obviously that was your sister. Wouldn't my stepmother love to know she was the one who brought them together?"

Again they were quiet, each of them caught up in their own memories. "There was never anyone else after she came home," Savannah murmured. "I'd catch her sometimes, lost in her thoughts, and I knew she was thinking about him. I just never knew who *him* was."

A soft rasping sound filled the air as Jake's fingers slid over his bristled chin. "Jessica found this picture with some books and papers after J.T. died. It's the only photo we have of him smiling after my mother died."

Savannah stared at the man in the photograph, knowing that Angela had taken this picture. "She loved him, you know."

The quiet passion in Savannah's voice pulled Jake from his reflection. He became suddenly, keenly, aware of the smell of peaches drifting from her damp skin and hair. The scent was as sweet as it was seductive, as soft as it was powerful, moving over him, stroking him like invisible silken fingers. Desire, hot and sharp, pumped through his body, heightening his senses. He had a wild crazy need to brush the damp golden hair from her neck and taste her there. It took every ounce of willpower he possessed to keep his hands at his sides.

"Would a woman leave a man she truly loved?" he asked, leaning closer. "And take his child without telling him?"

The heat of Jake's body burned through the thin cotton robe Savannah wore. She felt his breath fan her ear and slide down her neck, and her own breath caught in her suddenly tight throat. "Maybe he sent her away," she whispered.

Jake shook his head. "The Stone men never let go of what belongs to them."

It was a completely chauvinistic, utterly arrogant statement. Savannah should have laughed at the absurdity of it, but instead, her heart began to race. Wasn't it what every woman truly wanted? To be loved so deeply, so absolutely, that a man would never let her go? To be possessed by one man, knowing he would die to protect her? Fantasy, she chided herself. Ridiculous.

She pulled her robe tightly around her and turned so she wouldn't brush against Jake. The only problem was, her back was against the wall now. She looked up at him, determined not to react to his closeness. His eyes, dark as blue midnight, skimmed over her throat and rested on her breasts. She couldn't stop the thrill that leapt through her.

She wouldn't let him get to her. She *couldn't*. She needed a clear head and heart when it came to Jake and the rest of the Stone family. They had the power to take away the one thing in the world she loved: Emma. She couldn't let herself forget that for one minute.

"You're living in the Dark Ages, Jake Stone." She forced a cool smile. "Or should I say the Stone Age? Maybe it was that egotistical attitude that sent my sister packing. It's far from attractive, you know."

It was his turn to smile now. "Are you cold, Savannah?" he murmured. "You're trembling."

Her fingers clenched at the knot of her robe's belt. "I'm angry. You're passing judgment about a person and situation you know nothing about."

He stared at her for a long moment. "Maybe you're right," he finally conceded. "Maybe we both have a few things to learn. Questions to be answered. After all," he said huskily, "we both want the same thing, don't we?"

Jake's masculine scent assailed Savannah's senses. His voice stroked her like a lover's experienced hand. "And what's that?" she asked, blinking slowly.

He smiled and backed away. "The best for Emma, of course."

She felt ridiculous, nearly swooning because he'd moved too close. At least she could breathe now. She had to remember to keep her distance, that was all. "That's the only thing I want, Jake. Don't forget it. Now, if you'll excuse me, I'd like to say good-night to Jessica and Jared."

Jake raised one eyebrow. "That might be a little difficult. They left while you were in the shower."

"Left?" Savannah turned her head toward the living room and realized it had been awfully quiet. "For where?"

"Jessica works in Cactus Flat at the youth center and has a place there. Jared lives in a trailer on his own property." He looked at her curiously. "Did you think they lived here?"

A sharp tight knot formed in the pit of Savannah's stomach. "Well, I—I sort of assumed..."

Jake's brow furrowed. "Does that frighten you, being here alone with me?"

"No," she answered too quickly. "It's just that I, well, I hadn't..." She lifted her gaze to his. It was ridiculous to lie. "Yes."

He took a step back. "I don't want you, or Emma, to ever be afraid of me. You're both safe here, Savannah. I promise you that."

He looked at her for a long moment, then said good-night and turned toward the living room.

Savannah slowly let out her breath and watched him walk away. *Does that frighten you, being here alone with me?*

She wondered what he would say if she told him that it wasn't him she was frightened of, but herself.

Four

Hands on his hips, Jake stood at the edge of the bog and scowled at the steer. It was stuck in the thick mud clear up to its underside—the fifth one he'd come across today—and by far the worst.

The sky was clear at the moment, but for the past three days it had rained steadily, turning the area into a huge mud hole. Jake had always been careful to keep this section of land fenced off, but somehow the fence had gone down, and several head had managed to gain entrance. It was pure luck that he'd managed to get to them before they'd succumbed to the weather or wolves. More than luck. It was a miracle. With his finances as shaky as they were, even one steer lost might tip the scales irrevocably. One more setback and the bank "wolves" would be moving in on him.

With a weary sigh, Jake walked back to his horse and slipped the rope off the saddle. He'd been in and out of bogs since dawn and was covered with mud, but he'd managed to free all of his unfortunate victims without problems. If his

luck held out, he'd have this steer free and be home in time
to join Emma and Savannah for lunch.

Four days had passed since that night he and Savannah
had stood in the hall and looked at pictures. He'd managed
to spend some time with Emma, but other than dinner, he'd
kept a polite distance from Savannah. It seemed the safest
strategy, considering he couldn't get close to the woman
without wanting to argue with her or kiss her. Either one
would probably have her packing her bags, so he'd been as
cautious as a naked man climbing a barbwire fence.

But he thought about her far too much. Like now, when
he was trying to work, and at night—especially at night—
after he'd gone to bed. He wondered if she was asleep on the
other side of the wall. How her body might fit to his. If she
felt as soft as she looked . . .

The steer bawled at him. Jake swore back at it and tossed
the rope around its neck, then tied the other end to the saddle. Now came the good part, he thought irritably, stepping into the muck to make his way to the animal. He
worked quickly, moving from the back of the steer to the
front, digging away the quicksand from the legs.

"Looks like fun."

Startled, Jake twisted around at the sound of Savannah's
voice behind him. The steer chose that exact moment to
lurch sideways, knocking him off-balance. Swearing loudly,
Jake went down on his rear end and sank into the soft mud.
It oozed through his gloved fingers, then sucked at his hands
as he pulled them loose.

Furious, he stood slowly and faced Savannah. She was
mounted on Rosemary, a chestnut mare that Jessica rode.
"What the *hell* are you doing here?"

Eyes wide, she smothered a laugh as she stared at him,
taking in the thick layer of mud that covered him from the
waist down. In contrast, her long-sleeved cotton blouse was
Sunday-school white, her jeans, department-store blue.

Even the hat she wore looked as if it had just been taken out of its box.

"I'm sorry," she said. "I thought you heard me ride up."

Maybe he would have if he hadn't been so busy wondering what her skin would feel like under his hands. "You thought wrong," he growled, reaching for the lead line.

"Can I do something for you?" she asked hesitantly, moving her horse closer to the edge of the bog.

If he told her the first answer that came to his mind on *that* question, she definitely wouldn't like the answer, he thought fiercely. "You've done enough for the moment," he said, instead, swiping a huge glob of mud from his thigh.

Savannah winced as the dark lump of wet earth landed beside her horse. Biting her bottom lip, she looked contritely at Jake. "I really am sorry."

Jake had to drag his gaze from the sight of her worrying her bottom lip, or he knew he'd end up on his butt in the mud again. "Forget it." He worked his boots free from the bog. "Where's Emma?"

"Jessica came by and took her into town for lunch and an ice cream. They should be back by dinner."

He turned away and signaled his horse to back up, tightening the rope. The steer twisted its head, resisting the pull of the line. "Why didn't you go with them?"

"I thought they might like some time to themselves, and besides, it's too nice a day to sit in a car. I used to ride a lot when I was in college and I've missed it. Jessica said you wouldn't mind if I rode Rosemary."

Jake dug at the mud holding the steer's front legs. "This area is a little out of your way for a leisurely ride."

Rosemary sidestepped as she swung her head around to bite at a fly. Savannah tugged on the reins to steady the horse. "Since I was going to be out riding, anyway, Jessica pointed me in this direction and asked if I'd tell you that Mr. Williams called."

Damn! Williams was the loan manager at Midland First Federal, the bank that held the mortgage on the ranch. Despite the fact that Myrna's father held a considerable interest in the bank, the manager had given Jake no leeway at all. Jake had been putting the man off for the past two months, but it was getting more difficult by the day. He'd have to deal with the bank soon, but for the moment, between a bogged steer and a sexy blonde, he more than had his hands full.

Jake glanced up at Savannah as he tossed another glob of mud. She'd tucked up her hair under her hat, and a few stray golden curls swirled around her long slender neck. His throat tightened at the sight.

"Stone Creek is not the local equestrian center, Savannah," he snapped. "You could have gotten lost wandering around. What would you have done if you'd run into a rattlesnake or a pack of wolves?"

Her lips thinned as she straightened in the saddle. "Jessica gave me specific directions. And I doubt that a rattlesnake or a wolf would be any more irascible than you."

The steer bawled again, jerking its head as Jake yanked on the rope. "Oh, you'll excuse me," Jake said between clenched teeth. "I lost my charm in the mud somewhere."

"I said I was sorry." Savannah lifted her chin. "It's just a little mud, for heaven's sake. I don't really see what you're making such a fuss abou—"

The steer broke loose unexpectedly, knocking Jake backward into the mud again. The frightened animal then ran straight at Savannah's horse. The chestnut reared. Savannah screamed as she flew from the saddle.

And landed flat on her back in the mud beside Jake.

She was too horrified to move. She stared up at blue sky, felt the wet mud creep between her arms and legs. Jake leaned over her, his deep blue eyes dancing with devilment.

"I forgot to mention runaway steers and bog holes in my list of warnings," he said, and his broad grin nearly blinded her.

He thought this was funny! Damn him! Savannah tried to rise, but the mud sucked her back down.

Jake rose to his feet, then pulled off a mud-covered glove. "Need a hand?"

Fuming, Savannah brushed his hand away and struggled to free herself. Jake chuckled, then pulled himself from the bog and released the line on the steer. It trotted off, oblivious to the trouble it had caused.

Savannah had managed to pull herself to a sitting position when a pair of strong arms suddenly reached for her. Gasping, she had no choice but to wrap her arms around Jake's neck as he slipped his hands behind her knees and lifted her.

She stared down at her new clothes. "How will I ever get these clean?" She groaned. "How will I ever get *myself* clean?"

"It's just a little mud, for heaven's sake," Jake mimicked.

Savannah narrowed her eyes. "Put me down."

"My, my." Jake clucked his tongue. "I see you've lost your charm, too. Maybe you'd like to go back and look for it." He held her over the bog.

Savannah shrieked and clung to Jake's neck. "All right, all right. I'm sorry."

Terrified he'd drop her, Savannah burrowed herself into Jake's chest. The front of his shirt was still relatively clean and she turned her face into the cotton fabric, squeezing her eyes tightly shut. She felt the rumble of laughter before she actually heard it, and when it finally burst forth, she lifted her face and glared up at him. "What's so funny?"

"The look—" his words came out between bellows of laughter "—on your face when you landed in the bog...."

She felt the muscles in his chest ripple as he continued to laugh. "I imagine it was something like the look on *your* face when you fell in," she said, blowing a strand of hair from her eyes. "Sort of like you sat on a porcupine. I declare, I think that cow even felt sorry for you."

They both laughed then, standing on the edge of the mud hole, his arms around her. The horses watched them, and the steer wandered over to a nearby tuft of grass and dug in.

Jake couldn't remember the last time he'd laughed with a woman. He couldn't even remember the last time he'd held a woman in his arms. He stared into Savannah's meadow green eyes and felt something—something he was unfamiliar with, something he chose not to examine. And then it was gone as quickly as it came and in its place came a need. A need he understood only too well.

He wanted this woman. An ache spread through him as strong as it was urgent. He had to taste her, to feel her lips under his. His laughter died away as he held her gaze, and when he turned his attention to her lips he felt her go still. Her breathing turned shallow.

"Jake," she said quietly, "you can put me down now."

"Sure." He let her body slide down his with agonizing slowness. Her eyes turned smoky green as her breasts moved over his chest. Instinctively his hands cupped her bottom as he lowered her to the ground. *Damn,* but she felt good. So incredibly good. The ache in his body intensified and his heart raced.

This couldn't be happening, Savannah thought dimly. It had to be a dream. It *felt* like a dream. She was floating in a cloud of sensation, aware only of the feel of Jake's solid chest and the tightness of her breasts as her body pressed against his. Her hands slid over his arms and she felt the ripple of hard muscle beneath her fingers. She lifted her gaze to his, and the dark intensity of his eyes nearly took her breath away. He lowered his head, and with a will of their own, her lips parted and her eyes drifted closed.

His mouth was gentle on hers, his lips hot. Pleasure streaked through her, a sharp spiral of emotion that had her mind racing and her body humming. She whimpered softly, pressing herself closer, meeting the velvet thrust of Jake's tongue with her own. Her fingers curled around the fabric where his shirt opened, and she felt his flesh burn against her hands. Control slipped away and in its place came an urgency that consumed her.

Jake slanted his mouth against Savannah's and the kiss grew harder, deeper. She felt the moan that rose up from his throat, and the sensation excited her all the more. She should have been shocked, not only by her reaction to Jake's kiss, but by his arousal pressed so blatantly against the juncture of her thighs. But she wasn't. She was thrilled. Anticipation coiled tightly inside her and she shuddered from the force of it.

Jake felt the shudder move from Savannah's body into his own. Blood pounded in his temples. He wanted her. Now. Here. Desire throbbed through his body, screaming at him to take this woman and ease his pain. His lips moved over hers, hard and demanding, desperately, needing her closer. She welcomed him, meeting the hot thrust of his tongue with her own.

But even as he deepened the kiss he cursed himself. Not only for his timing, but because he knew what she tasted like now. Sweeter than anything he could have imagined. One taste would never satisfy him. It would never be enough.

The sun beat down on the back of his neck. It would be one hell of a sunburn, he thought darkly, but it would be worth it. If she was any other woman, he wouldn't even think twice.

But she wasn't any other woman. She was Emma's aunt. And after the physical satisfaction there was nowhere for this to go. There was no place for a woman like Savannah in his life. There was no place for *any* woman in his life beyond a night's pleasure. Or in this case, he thought in extreme frustration, an afternoon's pleasure.

Reluctantly he tore his mouth from hers and let her slide to the ground. The movement was sheer torture for him, and he held back the groan deep in his throat. He looked down at Savannah. Her passion-glazed eyes opened slowly, and her lips, still wet and parted, nearly had him reaching for her again. Sweat beaded on his brow as he stepped away.

Confusion filled Savannah's eyes. She stared at him, then blinked several times. He stood rigid, watching as awareness slowly returned to her face. Her cheeks flamed red.

A hawk shrieked overhead. Waves of heat shimmered off the hard flat ground. The rich earthy smell of the land permeated the air.

"You lost your hat," she said quietly.

He nodded slowly. "So did you."

They locked gazes for a long moment without speaking, then turned away from each other, both of them realizing they'd lost a great deal more than their hats.

"Jake, you're not being reasonable."

With his back to his stepmother, Jake stared out his living room window. Clouds framed the distant mountains, and he hoped like hell it wasn't going to rain again. He'd had enough mud today to last him a lifetime. He turned his head at the sound of the shower shutting off. Savannah had insisted on using the bathroom after him. He thought of her in there now, her skin glistening as she rubbed the towel over her—

"Jake, are you listening to me?"

Sighing inwardly, Jake turned and faced Myrna. Now that she'd hired someone to drive her around, God only knew how often she'd drop in unannounced. Legs crossed, she sat stiffly in the worn leather armchair that had been J.T.'s favorite. Dust spotted the front of her navy blue pants and she brushed it delicately away.

"There's nothing to listen to," he said dryly. "I have no intention of selling this ranch. Not to you or anyone else."

Myrna tapped her red-polished nails impatiently on the arm of the chair. "Why do you insist holding on to a non-profitable venture? You risk losing it all if you don't get out while you can."

Myrna was every bit Carlton Hewitt III's daughter, Jake thought bitterly. All either of them saw was the bottom line of a financial statement. The land itself, the sweat and blood that had been poured into it, meant nothing.

There was a graveyard under an oak tree that embraced every deceased Stone for the past 130 years, and the turned soil had barely settled on three of those graves. Jake would give it all away before he let Myrna have one square foot more than she already had her claws into.

"Ten years ago Stone Creek was the most profitable ranch in the county," he said flatly. "Strange how that all changed after J.T. married you."

Myrna lifted her chin indignantly. "Even J.T. would have known when to throw in the towel, Jake."

"There'd be no towel to throw in if he hadn't had to mortgage this place to build that monstrosity of a house you live in."

Cool disdain laced the look she threw him. "We could hardly live here with you. Daddy pulled a lot of strings at the bank so we could build our dream house. Your father loved Stone Manor every bit as much as I."

Jake nearly laughed out loud at the absurdity of her statement. J.T. had hated Stone Manor and had spent most of his time with Jake at the ranch.

Jake sighed. He was growing extremely weary of this conversation. "What would you do with this ranch, Myrna? Turn it into a shopping mall? No one besides you would drive this far to shop."

"All I have is the house." Myrna's voice was a near whine. "I have no land. Daddy's willing to offer you a great deal of money for this ranch—more than it's worth. We thought we might build some stables and hire a couple of trainers for some thoroughbreds. It would be fun.''

Fun? She wanted to buy the ranch so she could have *fun?* He counted slowly to ten. "No, Myrna," he said tightly. "I'm not selling.''

Exasperated, she let out a long breath. "Well, what about the child's land, then? You don't need it, and I'm sure the money will come in handy for both her and her aunt.''

Anger shifted, then settled in Jake's gut. He'd known it was only a matter of time before his stepmother tried to get her fingers in that piece of pie. "It's not for sale.''

"That's really not your choice, Jake. You might be the executor, but I'm sure the child's aunt has some say in the matter.''

"Her name is Emma," he ground out. "Emma Victoria Roberts Stone. And the land is *not for sale.*''

"What land?''

Jake turned sharply at the sound of Savannah's voice behind him. Wearing a blue cotton sleeveless dress, she stood in the doorway, her still-damp hair pulled into a French braid. Her cheeks were flushed from her shower and he felt a swift stab of desire as he remembered that same flush on her cheeks after he'd kissed her. *Damn it,* but his timing was consistently off with this woman.

Savannah paused before she entered the room. Jake and Myrna obviously hadn't heard her come in and the look of annoyance on Jake's face suggested he'd rather she left. But Emma's name had been mentioned, and what concerned her niece concerned her, as well.

Myrna smiled brightly. "Savannah. We were just talking about you.''

Savannah glanced at Jake. The tight expression on his face told her it wasn't a conversation he'd intended her to overhear. "Hello, Mrs. Stone.''

Gold bracelets jangled on Myrna's wrist as she reached over and patted the couch beside her chair. "Come sit down, dear. And please, do call me Myrna."

Savannah noticed the muscle that jumped in Jake's jaw as she moved hesitantly into the room. She also noticed the snug fit of the clean jeans he'd changed into and the contrast of tanned skin with the white shirt he'd rolled up at the sleeves. He folded his arms tightly, watching her as she sat on the couch, and for one brief instant she saw the hunger in his eyes. Her pulse skipped, then broke into a full run.

It was a good thing Myrna was here, Savannah decided. After what had happened between them this afternoon, she hadn't known how she was ever going to face him again. Neither one of them had spoken on the ride back in. Even as they'd unsaddled and taken care of the horses, not more than a dozen words had passed between them. How could she have lost control like that? What could she have possibly been thinking? But that was exactly the problem, she realized. She *hadn't* been thinking. At least, not with her head.

"I want to apologize for my behavior the other day, dear," Myrna said, interrupting Savannah's renegade thoughts. "I was just caught unawares, you understand."

The Stone men had a way of doing that to women, Savannah thought. "I realize that our stay here will be awkward for you."

"Not at all." Myrna gave a flick of her wrist. "In fact, it gives me an opportunity to get to know you both better. J.T. would have liked that."

Savannah glanced at Jake when she heard him mumble something under his breath. His narrowed eyes were a dark menacing blue, but he kept his mouth tightly closed. Why did he resent the woman so much? she wondered. Couldn't he see she was trying to be civil? Not that Jake would recognize "civil" if it bit him on the nose. Ignoring him, she turned back to his stepmother.

Myrna went on. "Why don't you and your niece come out to my place for lunch next week? I can have my cook put something special together for us."

Jake took a step forward. "I hardly think that's a good—"

"We'd love to." Savannah cut Jake off. She probably would have turned the woman down if he hadn't interfered.

"Wonderful." Smiling, Myrna rose and picked up her navy blue designer clutch purse. "William can pick you up early so we'll have time for a nice long chat."

Savannah offered a weak smile, already regretting her impulsive acceptance. "I'm sure that would be lovely."

Myrna walked by Jake. "Daddy always taught me not to let my sentiments get in the way of good business, Jake. Think about what we discussed."

He nodded stiffly, but did not answer her. After the woman let herself out, Jake turned to Savannah. Frustration etched lines around his eyes. "Why in the hell did you agree to have lunch with her?"

Savannah lifted her chin and leveled her gaze to his. "Let's just say it's my day to make mistakes."

Her verbal jab hit him square on the chin. His scowl deepened. "Myrna uses people to get what she wants, Savannah. That includes you and even Emma."

Was he any different? she wondered. "What could the woman possibly want from me or Emma? She knows nothing about us."

His expression hardened, but he said nothing, just turned his back to her and stared out the window.

"There is something, isn't there?" she asked, almost afraid to know. She took a step toward him, but knowing that she'd miscalculated the magnitude of her reaction to him before, she kept her distance. Still, she was close enough to smell the musky scent of his after-shave, and an involuntary shiver prickled her skin. "Jake, I think it's time you told me."

He turned to face her. "She wants land."

Savannah furrowed her brow. "What land? I don't have—" She stopped suddenly, remembering something that had made no sense to her before. "That first day we met you accused me of wanting land. I thought maybe you meant your ranch, but that isn't what you meant at all, is it?"

He shook his head. "When J.T. died, he divided Stone Creek in his will. Myrna got Stone Manor, but no land. The ranch went to me, an oil well to Jared, and a ghost town to Jessica."

Oil well? Ghost town? Savannah's eyes widened.

"There's another parcel," he went on. "It adjoins the ranch and backs up to Myrna's house. J.T. left that to Emma."

To Emma? J.T. left property to *Emma?* "But, how—" her voice faltered "—I mean, *why* would he do that?"

"Emma is J.T.'s daughter, but he was never able to be a father to her. The land was all he could give her."

She shook her head in bewilderment. "But he'd never even seen her. How could he know for sure that Emma was his?"

"He knew," Jake said with certainty. "He never would have left her the land if he didn't."

Savannah still couldn't believe it. Emma owned part of Stone Creek. "Exactly how much land are we talking about?"

"Ten thousand acres."

"Ten thousand acres!" She couldn't even comprehend that much land. Then the realization hit her. *He'd known all along.* But he'd said nothing, not one word. "When were you going to tell me this?"

Jake saw the distrust in Savannah's eyes as she stared at him. *Damn Myrna.* His stepmother had known exactly what she was doing when she came out here. "I'd planned on taking you and Emma out there on Sunday."

He watched her pace the length of the room. "What else do you have 'planned'?" she asked tightly.

He definitely didn't like the tone of her voice or the direction this conversation was taking. "I don't know what you're talking about."

Arms folded, she closed the distance between them. "Who's the executor of the estate?"

Jaw set tight, Jake ground out, "I am."

She lifted one eyebrow and gave an irritating, cocksure nod. "So you have control over the property?"

Jake set his back teeth, wondering how it was that this woman was able to incite such a range of emotions from him. Five minutes ago he'd wanted nothing more than to drag her to his bed. Now he was seriously entertaining the idea of throttling her. "Do you think you could get to your point sometime this year?"

"Ten thousand acres is a lot of land and a big chunk of Stone Creek. A nine-year-old child living in the big city wouldn't be interested in owning desolate ranch land. It must have worried you, not knowing if you'd find a For Sale sign on the property one day."

He held his growing anger in check. Barely. "I'd be notified in the event of a potential sale."

"But in the meantime you wouldn't know what the owner's intentions were. I'm sure you'd sleep better if you had the land's rightful owner close by, where you could keep an eye on her."

He almost laughed at that. He hadn't had a decent night's sleep since the day he'd brought them here. He narrowed his eyes in warning and took a step toward her. "Savannah, so help me—"

"Was that your plan for Emma, Jake?" she continued, his warning unheeded. "And me? Was I part of your plan, too? Did you think I'd fall for that Stone charm as easily as my sister?"

Something inside him snapped. He took hold of her shoulders. He watched her eyes widen, but defiance shone there, not fear. "You seem to forget your little performance that first day we met, Savannah, when you led me to believe you were Angela. It seems you had a plan of your own then."

"I would have said or done anything to protect Emma." She tried to twist out of his hold. "I still would."

"And so would I," he countered through gritted teeth. "My great-great-grandfather bought Stone Creek with a gold watch and two prize bulls. I wouldn't sell one foot of this land, let alone ten thousand acres. Maybe it's something you could never understand, but this land is our legacy, what we stand for, and that includes Emma, too.

"And as far as you and me, Savannah," he said, his voice rough as he pulled her against him and lowered his face within a whisper of hers. "I'll tell you right now I sure as hell wasn't thinking about Stone Creek or Emma this afternoon when I kissed you. I had one thought, and one thought alone—to have you in my bed, naked, with those damn sexy legs of yours wrapped around me."

Savannah knew she should be shocked by Jake's admission, but the only thing that shocked her was her reaction. His verbal image of their making love aroused her, as did his closeness. She went still, lifting her eyes to his. His blue eyes blazed with a dangerous mixture of desire and anger. His hands tightened around her arms.

There was no stopping this thing between them, and there certainly was no denying it. Her lips parted, waiting impatiently as he closed the breath of distance between them—

A horn honked repeatedly from outside, the sound growing louder as the car came closer. Swearing, Jake dropped his hands from Savannah and turned away. He dragged a hand through his hair and stalked to the window.

Saved by the horn, Savannah thought, drawing a deep breath as she folded her shaking arms in front of her.

A car door slammed, then Emma's laughter rang through the clear Texas air. "You-ou-ou can't catch me," she sang. "You can't catch me."

Emma burst through the front door, followed closely by Jessica, who scooped up the child and swung her. Emma wiggled out of Jessica's hold and took off again, through the kitchen and out the back door. Jessica ran past Savannah and Jake. "Hi, guys. See you later."

Jake stared after his two sisters, listening to the sound of their play. His mouth set tight, he finally turned back to Savannah. "Tomorrow is Saturday and I have to go to town for supplies. I'll take you and Emma out to the land on Sunday after I get the animals fed."

He grabbed his hat off the peg by the front door and jammed it on his head. The front door slammed behind him.

Savannah stared at the closed door for a long minute, wondering what in the hell she'd gotten herself into.

Five

Emma and Savannah rode in to town with Jake on Saturday, with Emma chattering the entire way about Betsy, the calf she'd been bottle-feeding. Excitement danced in the child's eyes as she told them that Jessica was going to help her enter the animal in the Cactus Flat Roundup. Savannah was thankful for her niece's incessant conversation. It not only filled the silence, it eased the tension.

She and Jake had not discussed Emma's property since Myrna's visit three days earlier. In fact, they'd barely seen each other for more than a few minutes. Jake was gone before the sun even rose and wasn't home till well after dark. He'd eat whatever Savannah left for him, then tuck Emma in and read her a story. Last night he'd even fallen asleep in the chair beside Emma's bed. Savannah had walked in and found him like that, the book hanging loosely in his hands and his head forward. Emma was sound asleep, as well, and the picture of the two of them brought a tightness to her chest.

She glanced at Jake now, watching him as he tilted his head toward Emma, patiently listening as the child described in animated detail her encounter with a mouse in the barn. He seemed truly interested, but was it all part of a plan? Had Emma's visit been a carefully orchestrated strategy on Jake's part to gain control of her land, or had he sincerely wanted to become acquainted with his newly found sister? Though he'd never said so, she knew he was having financial problems. He'd admitted he would do whatever he had to in order to keep his land and family together. Did that include manipulating a nine-year-old child?

"Aunt Savannah." Emma tugged on her sleeve. "Can we buy a bell for Betsy after we go to the grocery store?"

Savannah saw the corner of Jake's mouth twitch. "Maybe Jake can tell us where we can find one."

"I need to stop at the feed store when we get into town." Jake grinned down at Emma. "How 'bout you come with me and you can pick one out?"

Emma's face lit up and Savannah had to rein in the rush of emotion that swept over her. She didn't want to believe that Jake would use Emma to keep Stone Creek intact, but when it came to a man like Jake, denial was a dangerous thing. She couldn't afford to let herself be caught off guard.

Cactus Flat was a town straight out of an Old West travel catalog—right down to the wooden sidewalks and general store. The Cactus Flat Motel boasted twenty rooms with cable TV and the adjacent Bronco Diner boasted the biggest steak in west Texas. In front of the bank, two weathered-looking cowboys waved to Jake as he drove by, and in front of the beauty parlor an attractive redhead smiled, her gaze following them down Main Street. Much to Savannah's annoyance, she found herself wondering who the redhead was.

Jake parked in front of a small café called the Hungry Bear, and the scent of grilled hamburgers had Savannah's stomach growling as they stepped out of the truck. Jake suggested they eat before they picked up supplies, and Savannah quickly agreed.

The counter stools were nearly full and cowboy hats turned in unison as Jake entered the café. The pretty waitress pouring coffee from behind the counter looked up, her large brown eyes widening as she stared at Jake. "Hey!" a cowboy yelled, startling the waitress, who realized she had overfilled the man's coffee cup. Apologizing, she grabbed a towel and cleaned up the mess, her gaze darting toward the corner table where Jake had pulled out chairs for Savannah and Emma.

Ignoring another cowboy's request for a refill, the waitress hurried over to the corner table with a coffeepot in her hand. "Hi, Jake. Haven't seen you for a while."

Savannah detected the note of disappointment in the woman's tone. Jake nodded at the waitress as she poured him a cup of coffee, but did not respond to her comment. "Loretta, this is Savannah Roberts and my sister Emma."

Loretta's eyes narrowed in confusion as she glanced at the child. Emma, fascinated by a stuffed, seven-foot brown bear in the opposite corner of the café, was oblivious to the introduction.

"Your...sister? But—"

"Jake!" A gravelly voice rang out. "Jake Fitzgerald Stone! Come here so I can whup your butt!"

Savannah stared in amazement as an older man nearly as tall as Jake rounded the counter. His hair was as silver as his mustache and he had the lean muscular body of a man who kept himself in top physical condition. Savannah held her breath as the man approached angrily, his meaty fists swinging at his sides.

Jake lifted his coffee cup lazily to his lips. "How's it goin', Digger?"

"Don't you 'how's it goin'' me, you mangy prairie dog. You ain't made good on our last poker game." The old man waved a piece of paper under Jake's nose. "Two bucks, mister. Pay up."

Jake pulled the money out of his pocket. "Digger, you're as mean as that bear over there and stuffed with the same sawdust."

Digger grabbed the bills from Jake's hand and shoved them into his pocket. "Since your daddy couldn't teach you no respect, looks like I'll have to take the job. Come on out back where these here ladies won't have to watch you embarrass yourself."

Savannah gasped when Jake stood and stepped closer to the man. She sighed in relief when they threw their arms around each other. *Men are such imbeciles,* she thought.

"Digger, this is Savannah Roberts," Jake said when the old man released him. "Savannah, this is Francis Elijah Montgomery."

"You call me that again, boy, and I'll kick you so far you won't have to drive home."

It started up again between them, the exchange of insults, until Savannah didn't know whether to laugh or groan. Digger was in the middle of a comment comparing Jake's face to a jackass when he stopped suddenly. He stared at Emma, who was watching the two men in wide-eyed amazement.

Jake glanced at Emma, then met the old man's pale blue eyes. "This is Emma."

He said the words quietly, but gave no explanation. He obviously didn't have to. Digger stared at Emma, then a slow smile spread over his deeply lined face. He knelt down and waved the child to come. Emma glanced at Savannah, who nodded her approval. Hesitantly Emma scooted out of her chair and moved closer. She stood in front of the gruff old man, shifting her weight from one foot to the other.

"Your daddy was a good friend of mine," Digger said softly.

"He was?" Emma smiled widely.

Digger nodded. "Maybe sometime you and me can talk about him. I know he'd be right pleased if I passed along a few things to you he wanted you to know."

Moisture glistened in the old man's eyes, and Savannah felt her own eyes burn as she watched Emma nod enthusiastically. The child had asked questions about her daddy since she'd been three, but Angela had always said, "When you're older, sweetie." Well, now she was older, and she had no mother *or* father.

Digger laid a gentle hand on the child's shoulder, then stood and looked solemnly at Jake. "You take care of her, Jake. J.T. would have wanted that."

Jake nodded. "I intend to."

What did he mean by that? Savannah wondered. No one was taking care of Emma but her. She'd made that crystal clear. But then, *some* people were thickheaded, she thought, looking at Jake.

The waitress was looking at Jake, too, Savannah noted, and the look said she'd like to serve him more than coffee. Had Jake and she dated? Had he kissed this waitress the same way he'd kissed her? She'd lain in bed for the past three nights thinking about that damn kiss and the way she'd reacted to him. And no matter how much she denied it, no matter how much it embarrassed and infuriated her, she wanted him to kiss her again.

Digger refused Jake's money when he attempted to pay for the lunch and told him he'd win it off him the next poker game, anyway, so it didn't much matter. After a few more exchanged digs at each other, Jake drove them all to the feed store.

Savannah and Emma deliberated the purchase of a bell for Betsy while Jake ordered supplies. Emma insisted on a careful testing of every bell, and Savannah winced as her niece rang each one several times.

"I'd take that one," a deep voice said.

Savannah turned abruptly. A dark-haired man stood at the end of the aisle, his thumbs looped lazily in the waistband of his jeans. He grinned at Emma, then nodded to Savannah. "I had a teacher in the fifth grade that used to call us to class with a bell like that."

"I'm going to be in the fifth grade." Emma took hold of Savannah's hand. "And my aunt Savannah is a teacher."

"Really?" The man's dark brown eyes flashed to Savannah. "And is this your aunt Savannah?"

Savannah shifted uncomfortably as the man's gaze slid over her. He was handsome, she noticed, but his looks were more reminiscent of a corporate executive than a rancher. He moved toward them, his hand extended. "Sam McCants. I own the Circle B just west of here."

"Savannah Roberts." His hand was smoother than Jake's, Savannah noted as she placed her fingers in his palm. He wasn't as tall, either, but he was still over six feet. He held her hand a little longer than she would have liked. "And this is Emma."

"What's going on, Sam?" Jake asked flatly as he walked up beside them. His gaze dropped to Sam's hand on Savannah's, and she could have sworn she saw his jaw tighten. Sam let go, but the two men did not shake hands.

"Where you been keeping yourself, Jake?"

The way everyone was acting, Savannah was beginning to wonder if Jake had been hibernating for ten years.

"I've been around," he replied matter-of-factly.

Sam looked at Savannah and Emma. "These two ladies with you?"

"That's right."

"You always did get the pretty ones." Sam winked at Emma, then smiled at Savannah. Jake stiffened.

"We're just visiting," Savannah explained when Jake seemed reluctant to do so.

"Jake's my brother," Emma announced proudly.

Sam's brow raised. "Your brother?"

"That's right." Jake met the other man's curious stare, but gave no further explanation.

Why was Jake being so brusque? Savannah wondered. She didn't have a sense that he truly disliked Sam. He just didn't seem to want to talk to him.

"I've herded your steers out of my southwest section twice in the past week," Jake said tightly to Sam.

Sam shook his head. "I've fixed that fence four times this last month." He sighed with exasperation. "I'll send a hand over to take care of it."

"See that you do."

Sam turned back to Savannah. "I'm having a barbecue next week. I'm sure Jake would like to bring you and Emma. You can meet a few people and there'll be other kids there for Emma to meet."

"Will you have games?" Emma asked hopefully.

"And dancing, too." Sam looked at Savannah. "I insist on the first one."

Savannah glanced at Jake and saw the muscle in his jaw twitch. "Thank you," Savannah said, returning Sam's smile, "but I'm afraid I'm not much of a dancer."

"Well, then, I guess I'll just have to teach you," Sam offered.

Savannah felt Jake stiffen beside her when Sam took her hand again. "See you next week, then," he said, and tipped his hat. He smiled as he added, "If not before."

"Let's go." Jake grabbed Savannah's arm and practically dragged her to the counter. His shoulders were tight and his expression hard. After the clerk wrapped the bell, Jake handed it to Emma and she ran out to the truck with it. Hoisting a bag of grain over his shoulder, Jake stalked out of the store.

Exasperated, Savannah folded her arms and followed Jake out to the back of the truck. "Do you want to tell me what that was all about?"

"I don't know what you're talking about."

"You know damn well what I'm talking about. Something, or someone, put a bee in your bonnet. You were rude to your friend in there and you didn't even explain Emma or me."

"I don't have to explain my family to anyone," Jake replied tersely.

Savannah kept her voice down so Emma wouldn't hear. "Are you embarrassed about Emma?"

"Oh, for—" He threw the burlap bag into the bed of the truck, then faced her, his hands on his hips. "Why in the world would I be embarrassed about Emma?"

"This is a small town, Jake. Maybe it bothers you to admit to everyone your father had an affair."

He rolled his eyes. "Why would I bring Emma out here at all if that was true?"

That was exactly what Savannah wanted to know. Why *had* he brought Emma here? "You didn't introduce her to Sam as your sister, and you made it obvious you didn't want to take us to the barbecue."

"You really think I give a damn what anyone thinks?" He lowered his voice, but his tone was iron-hard. "Did you ever consider the fact that maybe I don't want to share what little time I have with Emma? That maybe I'd rather get to know my sister without two hundred people around?"

She hadn't thought of that. If it was true, it was certainly a good reason. And he *had* introduced Emma to the waitress. Savannah suddenly felt very foolish.

"And as far as Sam goes," Jake went on, "I've known him all my life, and I know exactly why he invited you to the barbecue. It had nothing to do with Emma meeting other children and everything to do with the way you look in those tight jeans of yours."

Of all the... Savannah felt her cheeks flame, and when she started to turn away from him he grabbed her wrist.

"Oh, no, you don't." Jake kept his back to the cab of the pickup so Emma couldn't see them. "You wanted to hear my reasons, and the minute you don't like what I say you think you can walk away. You're going to listen, whether you like it or not."

She pressed her lips together and met his dark gaze.

"Maybe you're too naive to see it, Savannah, but Sam just gave you every indication he was interested in a very different kind of dancing than you thought." His hand tightened on her wrist as he pulled her closer to him. "Just remember this, for however long you're here, Emma's not the only person I have no intention of sharing."

He released her and stormed back into the feed store. Savannah watched him go, her heart pounding furiously against her rib cage. *Emma's not the only person I have no intention of sharing.* Good Lord, had he really said that?

What a ridiculous, overbearing, macho thing to say. She wasn't his to share or not share with anybody, Savannah thought indignantly. Just who did he think he was?

She glanced over her shoulder toward the feed store, rubbing the tingling sensation that lingered on her wrist. It was going to be a long three weeks, she thought, dragging in a slow breath to steady her nerves.

A very long three weeks.

Emma's land was close to the base of mountains that Savannah had only seen in the distance from Jake's ranch. Jake pulled the pickup under a stand of cottonwood, then shut off the engine and came around to open the door for Savannah and Emma. Emma, delighted they were having what she considered a fun Sunday picnic, ran off to a nearby stream at the base of a ravine where yellow and white wildflowers sprinkled the banks. The sun, nearly overhead, promised to scorch the sparse land, but for the moment a cool breeze kept the heat to a minimum.

"It's beautiful," Savannah murmured, watching her niece throw pebbles into the shallow water.

"Right here it is." Jake pulled off his denim jacket and tossed it into the bed of the truck. "But most of this land is flat and rocky. I use it for grazing, but it's not good for much else."

"So you'd lose grazing land if it were sold," Savannah said bluntly.

His face hardened. "Don't try and read between the lines on everything, Savannah. You're getting downright paranoid."

Maybe she was. And maybe she had reason to be. But for the moment, she decided to put her mistrust of Jake on hold. This was a lovely spot and Emma was having a good time. Savannah didn't want to spoil her niece's afternoon by arguing with Jake.

"All right," she said. "Let's call a truce for the afternoon. I'll get the sandwiches and iced tea and you get the blanket."

The tension between them eased for the moment. Jake spread a thick Indian blanket under the shade of a cottonwood while Savannah unloaded the basket she'd packed. A low rumble and cloud of dust in the distance caught Savannah's eye and she pointed to it. "What's that?"

Jake shaded his eyes and stared at the rising cloud. "Wild horses," he explained. "They've been here since my granddad ran this place. We leave them be."

She could see them now. There were probably twenty or so, various colors, and they seemed hell-bent to get somewhere. Her heart pounded harder as they drew closer. Without warning, they turned suddenly and headed in another direction. "They're beautiful," she breathed.

Jake nodded, but he was watching her, Savannah realized, and she blushed. Emma came running up then, pointing excitedly at the retreating horses.

Savannah set out the sandwiches and they ate in silence for a few minutes, listening to the sound of the breeze rustle the cottonwoods. A lizard darted out from behind a rock, and when it headed for the blanket, Jake tossed a pebble at it to deter it. Emma giggled, pointing at the reptile as it slithered away. Savannah shivered.

It amazed Savannah how well her niece seemed to fit in here. Atlanta was a different planet compared to Stone Creek. The land here stretched forever with very little green. There were no sidewalks to skate on, no other children to play with. Jake didn't even have a TV. And yet Emma was happier than Savannah had ever seen her. Savannah saw a bond forming between Emma and her new family, and it scared the hell out of her. Was it possible she might actually lose her niece?

No. She'd never let that happen. They'd be leaving in a few weeks, going back to their own home. Emma would settle down and start school again in the fall. She'd be with her friends and forget about this other part of her life, except for Christmas cards and birthdays. She'd probably even forget that calf she was so crazy about.

The peace Savannah had felt only a moment before was gone now. Doubt and apprehension filled her and she turned away to fill her glass with tea.

When she turned back, Savannah noticed that Emma was watching Jake as she chewed thoughtfully on a peanut-butter sandwich. Jake took a big swallow from a paper cup filled with iced tea as Emma leaned forward.

"Jake," Emma said, picking at a strand of hair that had stuck to her cheek, "how come you don't have a wife?"

He lurched forward, nearly choking on his drink. Tea spilled down the front of his blue shirt. Oblivious to her indelicate question, Emma persisted. "Well, how come?"

Savannah knew she should intervene and discourage Emma's question, but the truth was, she wanted to know herself. When Jake glanced sideways at her, she simply smiled.

Swiping at the front of his shirt, Jake answered irritably, "I had one."

Savannah glanced up in surprise. So he *had* been married. She wasn't sure why that surprised her, but it did.

"What happened to her?" Emma asked.

Savannah's good breeding insisted she interrupt. "Pecan, you mustn't ask—"

"That's all right." Jake cut Savannah off with a wave of his hand, then turned his attention to Emma. "I guess she liked money better than she liked me."

Emma frowned as she thought about what Jake said. "I had a friend once—Alexandra—and she was nice to me so she could come over and play with my Priscilla Princess doll. When my neighbor's dog chewed Priscilla's arm off, Alexandra didn't want to play with me anymore. Aunt Savannah said Alexandra wasn't a very good friend."

Jake looked at Savannah, his gaze intense. "No, Emma, she wasn't."

Though it was hard for Savannah to imagine a woman loving money more than a man, she realized that those kind of women were in abundance. She felt an unreasonable tug of anger at a faceless woman she'd never met.

Emma set her sandwich aside and brushed the crumbs off her hands. "Did you have any kids?"

Jake's face darkened at the question and Savannah realized it was definitely time to ward off the questions. "Emma, look—" she pointed toward the stream "—I think I see a rabbit."

Emma immediately scrambled up, then ran off, calling over her shoulder. "Save some cookies for me."

Savannah sipped on her iced tea in the awkward silence that followed Emma's departure. "I'm sorry," she said at last. "About your wife."

He shrugged. "It was a long time ago."

"But you've never remarried."

He shook his head. "Once was enough, thank you. I'll leave matrimony and kids to Jessica and Jared."

Savannah knew she was risking the truce they'd called, but she had to ask. "How does Emma fit into your life, Jake? Is she replacing children you'll never have?"

His hard gaze met hers. "Emma is my sister. My flesh and blood. If I had ten kids I'd never turn my back on her. And since you're suddenly so interested in talking about our personal lives," he added dryly, "why aren't you married?"

Annoyed with herself for pursuing this line of conversation, Savannah busied herself by repacking the lunch basket and stuffing the trash into a brown paper bag.

"I intend to," she answered stiffly. "Soon."

He'd moved closer to her on the blanket, and she felt the energy radiate from his body into hers. She stiffened when his breath fanned the back of her neck.

"You have someone in Atlanta?" His voice deepened.

Jake was staring at her mouth, Savannah realized, and her heart began to beat heavily, like a bass drum. "Not at the moment, but I'm sure something will come up."

So there was no one waiting for Savannah back home. Jake hated to admit it mattered to him, but for some reason, it did. The smell of peaches drifted to him and he breathed in deeply, dragging the scent into his lungs and holding it there. When he slowly released it, he watched her reach up and gracefully rake her fingers though her hair. Desire pulsed through his veins as he wondered what those fingers would feel like on his body. On his skin.

Damn, but it was getting hot.

He swiped the back of his hand over his temple and tipped his hat back. Something told him it was going to get a hell of a lot hotter.

At the sound of Emma's laughter, Jake glanced up and watched as Emma gathered more wildflowers.

"Is that how you do it in Atlanta?" he turned back to Savannah and asked, curious at her choice of words for finding a husband. "Wait for something to 'come up'?"

Savannah lifted one eyebrow and cast a sideways glance at him. "And I suppose you have a better way?"

"I have a better way, all right. Avoid the situation entirely."

Does he really mean that? Savannah wondered. He'd told her that lonely men make mistakes, and obviously he'd meant not only his father, but himself. "Would you really spend the rest of your life out here alone?" She waved a hand toward the mountains. "You wouldn't want to share all this with someone?"

"I never said anything about being alone. If the right woman came along, I'd be more than willing to share everything I have." Savannah felt Jake's intense gaze skim over her, and the look in his eyes brought a swirl of heat low in her stomach. "Especially my bed."

The deep sensuous tone of Jake's voice was like an electric current rippling over her skin. She realized she'd stopped breathing when he leaned back and said coolly, "Marriage just isn't part of the deal."

Stunned, Savannah stared at him. Did he think she'd be interested in that kind of arrangement? A mixture of hurt and outrage coursed through her. And another feeling, though she hated to admit it.

Disappointment.

Hands tightly gripping the bag in her hand, she stood and looked down at him. "I expect that's something similar to the deal J.T. offered Angela."

Eyes narrowed, Jake sat up straight. "We don't know anything about what my father offered your sister."

"Maybe not. But I do know what I can offer their child, besides love. A stable home life, a good education and someday a father figure she can look up to."

Father figure? Anger, as unreasonable as it was unexpected, surged through Jake. "Emma has two big brothers. She doesn't need any more of a father figure than that."

She laughed harshly. "I'll call and you can reprimand her over the phone when she misbehaves, or better yet, maybe you can videotape a weekly advice and lecture and mail it to me. We'll make popcorn every Friday night and watch it."

He rose stiffly, hands on his hips as he moved closer to her. "We'll work something out."

She faced him, arms folded. "There is no 'we,' Jake. It's Emma and me. We came here so you could get to know each other, not for you to tell us how to run our lives. We managed just fine before you and when we leave we'll continue to do so."

"Dammit, Savannah, for once can't you just—" He stopped and jerked his gaze upward. Eyes narrowed, he froze.

"What is it?" Savannah followed Jake's gaze.

She saw it then. In the distance, coming from the direction of the ranch.

A thick black curling cloud of smoke.

Six

Drought, wolves and fire were the stuff ranchers' night-mares were made of. Jake watched the black cloud of smoke grow bigger as they approached the ranch.

Don't let it be the barn, God. Please not the barn.

The animals would be trapped in there without anyone to help them out. The horses...Emma's calf.... He glanced down at the wide-eyed child beside him. Savannah, her own face pale, her eyes staring rigidly ahead, held her niece in the comfort of one arm. No one had spoken a word since they'd jumped into the truck.

Jake felt as if a steel band was closing around his chest. He white-knuckled the steering wheel and floored the accelerator. Each mile was a trip to hell and back, but finally he turned off the road, the truck fishtailing and sending a cloud of dust and rocks spinning from the back tires. As they swung sideways, Savannah held on tightly to the armrest with one arm and Emma with the other.

It wasn't the barn. He could tell that, even though they were still two miles away. Because there was so much smoke, he thought for a moment it might be the house, but as they grew nearer, he realized, with a second sigh of relief, that it wasn't.

What the hell was it?

As they neared the house, his question was answered. "It's the storage shed," he said, pointing to a small structure several hundred yards behind the house that was engulfed in flames. "I keep spare tires in there. That's why there's so much smoke."

Jake brought the truck to a screeching halt in front of the house and jumped out. The fire crackled and roared, swallowing the shed.

"Get the animals out of the barn," he yelled over his shoulder to Savannah as he ran toward the side of the house. "If the wind shifts and carries any sparks, the roof might catch."

Her heart pounding, Savannah watched Jake grab a high-pressure hose from the side of the house. He twisted the handle and a huge stream of water shot out from the wide nozzle.

Under strict orders not to move, Emma stayed in the truck while Savannah released the horses and Emma's calf into the corral. She was back at her niece's side within minutes, and they sat together in the cab and watched Jake fight the fire. Fortunately the shed was small and winds were light. The smoke turned gray, then almost white as the water doused the flames. Ashes fell like gray snowflakes and the stench of smoke and burned rubber singed the already hot air.

When nothing more than a steamy mist rose from the torched wooden structure, Jake signaled for Savannah to shut down the hose. Fists clenched at his sides, Jake approached the blackened, steaming shed and stared at it.

It could have been worse, he told himself, but neverthe-
less, frustration had him kicking the front door. The door
collapsed, falling inward. Part of the roof followed suit.
Damn!

Arms folded, Savannah stood next to Jake. "Was there
anything valuable in there?"

*When you're hanging on to a cliff by your fingernails,
even the tiniest pebble makes a difference.* He shook his
head slowly. "Spare tires for the equipment, some tools and
engine parts. Nothing that can't be replaced."

If he had the money. Which he didn't. Hell, he hadn't
even been able to keep the insurance policy current.

The sound of embers crackling and wood settling drifted
from inside the shed. "How did it start?" she asked.

Jake's frown deepened. "That's a good question. I
haven't been out here for a while. It's wired for electricity,
though. I suppose it's possible there was a short."

He didn't sound as if he believed that for a minute, Savannah thought, but she also thought it best not to question him on it. At least, not now. "I've got to get back to
Emma. She wants to make sure Betsy's all right."

He nodded. "I'll be here for a while cleaning up, then I'll
need to finish the chores I put off this morning. Tell Emma
I'm sorry we had to cut the picnic short."

Savannah saw the weary slump of Jake's shoulders. It
wasn't enough he had more work on this ranch than one
man could handle. Now he had to deal with this by himself.
She felt an overwhelming need to take him in her arms, but
she knew that he would consider any acceptance of comfort as a weakness. "What can I do?"

He shook his head. Soot and sweat covered his brow and
he swiped at his forehead with the back of his hand. "I've
got it under control. Go on and take care of Emma."

She started to walk away, then turned back. "Dammit,
Jake," she said, then quickly softened her voice. She

reached out and touched his arm. "Please. Let me help you."

Smoke trails curled around them as he studied her for a long moment. His gaze moved to her hand on his arm, and when he met her eyes again, his look was one of strained relief. "The three end stalls need cleaning and the horses could use some fresh water."

She smiled slowly, pleased that he was finally letting her help. She was coming to understand more each day why he loved this ranch and this land so much. When you had to fight so hard to keep something, when you knew you might lose it at any minute, it mattered more. It meant something beyond dollar signs.

She turned and walked back to the truck. She hadn't the foggiest idea how to clean out a stall, but she'd figure it out.

Jake sat in the quiet darkness of his office, the only light a single crookneck lamp spotlighting the papers strewn across his desk top. He stared at the column of figures he'd totaled three times, hoping each time that they'd change. They didn't.

With a heavy sigh, he leaned back in his chair and rubbed the bridge of his nose between his thumb and forefinger. It was two in the morning and he was no closer to a solution now than he was when he'd started five hours ago. It wasn't any one thing that was pushing him over the edge; it was a combination of everything. Fences down, sick animals, unexpected truck repairs, the fire today. He could deal with any one of those things separately. But combined, they were crushing him. It was slow, but just as effective. He was two months behind on the mortgage, three months behind on the tractor payments and extended to the limit with every supplier he dealt with. His savings were drained and the small sum of money J.T. had left him had just about run out.

He stared at the empty glass of whiskey in front of him and considered a refill. What the hell, he wasn't going to be much good for anything tomorrow, anyway. Why not go for broke? he thought, then laughed dryly at the expression. He *was* going broke.

Propping one leg up on his desk, he drew a deep breath and refused to give in to that possibility. He *would* hold on to Stone Creek, dammit. He just had to make it to the fall. This year's herd would bring in enough money to not only pay off his debts, but to finance some much-needed repairs around the ranch. And if he had a little left over, he mused, he could even take Savannah and Emma down to San Antonio for the Fall Festival. Emma would love the carnival, and Savannah would enjoy the—

What the hell was he thinking? Jake rubbed a hand over his face to clear his thoughts. Savannah and Emma wouldn't be here in the fall. They were leaving in two and a half weeks. Going back to Atlanta. To their fancy town house and fancy school.

The thought left a hollow feeling in his chest. He'd enjoyed Emma's being here. Maybe too much. He'd never realized how much he'd missed having children. His ex-wife came to his mind, and he had to close his eyes against the pain that shot through him. Her betrayal had been unforgivable. No woman would ever have that kind of hold on him again.

But he couldn't stop the image of Savannah that crept into his mind and his senses. He smiled, remembering how exhausted she'd looked this afternoon when he'd come into the barn. She was finishing the third stall, tossing hay in with a pitchfork. Her hair had hung in limp honey blond ringlets around her flushed face. When she stopped to wince at a blister on her hand, he watched her stretch, then arch her slender back, pressing her breasts tightly against her pink blouse. He'd stared at her, feeling as if a horse had kicked him in the gut. It made no difference that he was black from soot and ashes and she was covered with dirt and perspiration. He'd wanted—no, he'd *ached*—to lay her down in the fresh sweet hay she'd spread and cover her body with his.

He still ached, dammit.

He stared at his whiskey glass again. What the hell. It might be temporary, but he'd accept any comfort at the moment. He started to reach for the glass.

"Jake?"

The soft whisper nearly had him falling backward. He jerked his head up and saw her standing there, a shadowy curvy form in the doorway. He nearly groaned out loud. *Not now,* he thought with near desperation. He couldn't deal with this woman and what she did to him right now. It was too damn late and he was too damn tired.

"What is it?"

At the terse sound of Jake's voice, Savannah hesitated in the doorway, gripping the knot of her robe belt with cold fingers. The room was swathed in darkness, except for the desk lamp that illuminated Jake's denim-clad leg and scuffed boot. He hadn't moved, but she could see the outline of his tall form in the chair.

"Is something wrong?" he asked with more concern now, but he still hadn't moved.

"I was just going to get a drink of water and saw the light. I'm sorry, I didn't mean to intrude."

She didn't tell him she hadn't been able to sleep. That he'd invaded her dreams and her thoughts and if she'd had to lie in that bed one more minute with all that empty space around her, she just might go crazy.

He said nothing, and silence, except for the soft tick-tick of a clock somewhere, surrounded them. The tension stretched taut, closing around her. She found it hard to breathe and her pulse began to beat low and heavy.

She started to back away.

"Come here, Savannah."

Her heartbeat doubled at Jake's words. It was a command laden with sensuality. With desire. Her body responded at a level where she had no control. There was no logic here, no reason. Only raw open need.

She went to him.

"Give me your hand," he said roughly.

She stood beside him, just barely able to see the features of his face. Her throat was too dry to speak and her fingers shook as she did what he asked.

He dragged his leg from the desk, leaning forward as he took her hand. The coarse texture of his fingers on hers made her pulse skip. He turned her palm to the light and examined the blister between her thumb and forefinger.

"Have you put something on this?"

"It's all right," she whispered.

"You never know," Jake said huskily. "Once something gets under your skin, there's no telling what can happen."

He traced the lines on her palm with his thumb and Savannah felt her breasts tighten with anticipation. Heat coiled low in her stomach and settled between her thighs. She didn't stop him when he brought her hand to his mouth. When he pressed his lips to her palm, she closed her eyes.

"Savannah," he murmured, and his hot breath sent waves of desire coursing through her. "Do you know what you do to me? Do you know how much I want you?"

Yes, she wanted to scream. *As much as I want you.* But she couldn't speak. It would break the spell. She'd wake up and the dream would be gone. The mistrust would be back, the uncertainty. If she never spoke, then later she could pretend this had never happened.

His tongue caressed the sensitive skin on her palm and she bit the inside of her mouth to hold back the moan. When he moved upward, tracing the inside of her wrist, she did moan. An urgency grew between them and he circled her waist with his free hand, pulling her to him.

He drew her hand to his chest and slipped her fingers under the open fabric of his shirt. His skin burned where she touched him. "I've wanted to feel your hands on my skin since the first time I met you."

Savannah felt as if they were two wild animals, alone in the dark, driven by forces beyond their control. She withdrew her hand from Jake and their gazes locked while she untied the belt of her light cotton robe. He cupped her bottom with his hands and buried his face in her stomach. Murmuring his name, she raked her hands through his thick hair.

Never had she given herself so completely, so mindlessly to physical desire. Doubt and distrust melted away. Need consumed her, so sweet and so intense, she thought she might cry.

His hands slipped under her robe and pushed her short gown upward, exposing her to him. She arched toward him, gasping now as he slid both hands up her bare stomach and cupped her breasts. She moaned again as he took one swollen breast into his mouth and sucked the hardened nipple.

The light scratching of Jake's beard against her sensitive skin sent sensation after sensation rippling through her. She held tightly to him, digging her fingernails into the skin of his shoulders.

"Jake . . . Jake . . ." she whispered over and over.

"What, Savannah?" he murmured. "Tell me what you want."

"I . . ." She caught her lower lip between her teeth as he circled the peaks of her breasts with his thumbs. "I want . . ."

Those two words had her hesitating. What *did* she want? A one-night stand with a man who'd openly admitted he wasn't interested in anything but the physical side of love? A man who stood to gain a great deal by one simple conquest?

Her body said yes—screamed it—but her head said no. She couldn't do this. One sister falling for the Stone charm was enough. She remembered the pain Angela had gone through. Savannah was determined not to make the same mistake.

She stepped away, breaking contact between them and pulling her robe back together. "I shouldn't have come in here, Jake. What I want is something entirely different from what you want. I'm sorry."

He sat there for a moment in the shadows, unmoving. When he spoke at last, his voice was as weary as it was heavy. "I'm sorry, too."

Savannah knew if she stood there one more second she'd throw herself into his arms again. Without looking back, she turned and nearly ran from the room.

The Circle B Fourth of July barbecue was the event of the year for the town of Cactus Flat and all the neighboring ranches. Red-and-white-checkered tablecloths covered long buffet tables heaped with mounds of traditional holiday food: corn on the cob, hamburgers, hot dogs, barbecued ribs and enough potato salad to feed a hungry platoon of marines. The smell of the barbecuing food flavored the air, and a country western band played an assortment of favorite songs, ranging from Hank Williams to Garth Brooks. Red, white and blue banners and balloons decorated Sam McCant's landscaped patio area, and an ice-cream station was set up by the pool.

Stone Creek had once been as successful a ranch as the Circle B, but after Jake's mother had died, J.T. had seemed to lose interest in expanding. After he married Myrna, what money there was had been slowly eaten away by the woman's extravagant tastes.

Jake knew if he could hold on, it would only take a few short years before Stone Creek would be operating at full potential again. He could make the ranch what he and his father had always dreamed of.

If he could hold on. *That* was the problem.

The sound of laughter and talking brought Jake back to the present. It had been a long time since he'd been to a party. The collar of his black dress shirt felt too tight, his jeans too stiff. But determined to make the best of the day for Emma's sake, he drew a deep breath and placed a hand on Savannah's elbow as he guided her and Emma under an archway of paper streamers and balloons.

It was the first time he'd touched her since that night in his office almost a week before. He'd put in extra hours the past few days, not only to work off the frustration, but to keep his distance. He knew she'd been right to put an end to things before they'd gotten out of hand, but he also knew that if they were alone again, if even once he smelled the scent of peaches that always lingered on her skin, then he'd end up making a fool of himself. Again.

He looked at her now, dressed in a white ruffled blouse and short Western skirt that showed off her long legs. Legs that every man here would be looking at. His hand tightened on her elbow.

"Where'd you get those clothes?" he asked, suddenly irritated.

"Your sister loaned them to me. I didn't have anything appropriate for a party." She glanced down at what she'd worn. "Don't you like them?"

Like them? They showed every damn curve she had. He liked them so much all he could think about was taking them off. Jake made a mental note to have a chat with Jessica. "Jeans would have been fine."

Savannah frowned at Jake. Her pulse had skipped at his unexpected touch. She was well aware it was the first time he'd come within six feet of her in the past week. Since Jared and Jessica had spent a lot of time visiting, she hadn't been at a loss for company, but still, she'd been out of sorts all week. Wanting something she couldn't put a name to.

"Get ready for the onslaught," he warned, nodding to several people who were now looking their way.

Suddenly Savannah found herself surrounded by a group of men in Stetsons, clean jeans and a rainbow of Western shirts.

"Hey, Jake," one man said as he slipped a long-necked bottle of beer into Jake's hand. Another man slapped him on the back, then smiled and stared openly at Savannah. "Now we know why you been hiding out, Jake."

"I think Jessica is looking for you, Jake." A third, gap-toothed man had squeezed between the other two men. "How 'bout I show your lady around while you go see?"

"How 'bout we ask Mary if that's okay?" Jake returned, taking a pull from his bottle.

At the mention of his wife, the man looked sheepishly behind him.

Savannah's cheeks flamed at all the attention. Jake had kept his hand on her back, and though he laughed and joked with the other men, she felt the tension coiled inside him. With his fingers splayed possessively on her back, it was difficult for her to concentrate on the introductions, but she smiled and nodded, trying to ignore the response he elicited from her with the simplest touch.

Emma suddenly had a circle of children her own age surrounding her, as well. Several women joined in, eager to meet Jake's new sister and her aunt. When Emma ran off to play, Savannah finally allowed herself to relax. She realized she'd been worried about meeting these people and how they would treat her niece. But not one person had looked at Emma with anything other than a welcome smile. She'd been completely accepted.

"Savannah!"

Jessica waved from across the pool and hurried over. She gave Savannah a hug, then reached up and gave Jake a kiss on the cheek. He said something to her under his breath that made her laugh.

"Come on, Savannah." Jessica took Savannah's hand. "Let's get you away from my brother, the grouch. Maybe if he watches closely, he might learn how to have some fun."

Jake scowled at his sister, but said nothing as she hauled Savannah away. From then on, Savannah felt as if she was in a whirlwind. Jessica introduced her to nearly every man and woman there, careful to keep her away from Myrna, then loaded a plate of food, explaining every dish and whatever history might be attached to it. They drank beer, ate barbecued ribs and played several games of bingo, where Savannah won a handwoven basket filled with dried flowers and Emma won a game of jacks.

Dancing started when the sky turned a hazy shade of gray and orange. As the couples paired off, Savannah glanced at Jake and saw him break away from the group of men he was standing with. She felt her heart lurch as he made his way toward her, his eyes focused and intent.

She couldn't help but think how handsome he looked in his black dress shirt and shiny boots. Dark and dangerous. The way he moved emanated a masculinity few men could match, and his appeal radiated from a level that even chemists couldn't explain. Her own chemistry responded at that same level, and as their gazes met, her heart was pounding against her chest.

"Savannah?"

She jumped at the sudden voice so close to her ear. Beer splashed out of the glass she'd been sipping for the past hour. "Mr. McCants. You startled me."

"Sam." He smiled and took the glass from her hand. "We'll get you another one of these after we have that dance you promised me."

Hesitant, Savannah glanced at Jake again and saw the frown on his face. He was still moving toward her, but stopped when a woman stepped up and touched his arm. It was the redhead she'd seen in town that day.

Sam had already slipped an arm around her waist and was leading her toward the other dancers. *Why now?* she groaned to herself, trying to get a look at Jake. She couldn't possibly be rude to the host. Helpless, she forced a smile and moved onto the dance floor, managing to follow along with the fast two-step. She tried to break away when the music stopped, but he pulled her close as a waltz started.

"You move nice," Sam said, sliding his gaze over her.

"Thank you." *Jake! Where are you?*

Sam's hand tightened on her waist and subtly nudged their bodies closer. There was no doubt in Savannah's mind that Sam McCants had a stable full of women. He was handsome, obviously successful and extremely charming. But for some reason, he just didn't quite ring her bell, she thought, remembering their meeting in the feed store.

And that reason was Jake, she realized. She scanned the crowd for him again, but he was nowhere in sight.

"I thought you might like to come over one day this week and I'll show you around the ranch," Sam offered.

His expression told her the only place he'd like to show her was his bedroom. What could she say? It was pretty difficult to have a busy social schedule in the middle of nowhere. "Well, I—"

"My turn, Sam," a deep voice interrupted.

Grateful, Savannah turned. It wasn't Jake, but it was the next best thing. Jared. Reluctantly Sam released her, tipping his hat as he thanked her. His gaze stayed on them both as she stepped into Jared's arms and they danced away.

"You saved me," she whispered.

A half smile tilted one corner of Jared's mouth. "Actually it was Sam I was saving. I think Jake went looking for a gun when you started dancing with him."

"What's the problem between those two?" Savannah asked, remembering Jake's hostility toward Sam.

Jared shrugged. "Can't really say. Some things a man keeps to himself."

Something told Savannah that Jared had things he also kept to himself. Things that made his eyes lonely and his smile sad.

"Don't look now," he said, grinning as he twirled her, "but Jake's giving me the evil eye."

Savannah tried to see around Jared's wide chest, but he pulled her back. "What say we slip another burr under Jake's saddle?" he teased, whispering in her ear as if they were lovers. "Can't think of anything more fun than gettin' my big brother's goat."

She wanted desperately to see where Jake was, but Jared was moving around too much. "What makes you think it matters to Jake who I dance with?" she asked carefully.

Jared laughed out loud. "Lady, I'm tempted to call the fire department every time you two get within shoutin' distance of each other. You might be foolin' each other, but you're not foolin' anyone else."

Savannah felt her cheeks flame. Was it really that obvious? Could anyone just look at her and know how she felt about Jake? With a small groan, she laid her forehead against Jared's chest. "We're not even fooling ourselves, Jared. It just won't work."

"Don't make it more complicated than it is," Jared said, then dragged her against him. She actually saw a smile in his eyes. "He's watching. Look at me like you're madly in love. That will set his pot to boiling fast."

Jared dipped her suddenly and she held on tight, laughing at his outrageousness. She might be miserable inside, she thought with a sigh, but at least she was having fun on the outside.

Jake, on the other hand, wasn't having any fun at all. He leaned back against a patio column, arms folded, a bottle of beer in his hand, and tried to decide who he was going to kill first—Sam or Jared. Sam probably. He'd danced with Savannah first. Jake supposed he really shouldn't kill his own brother, though. It might not set well with Jessica or Emma.

Okay, he decided, taking a pull from his bottle, he'd just maim him.

Dammit, anyway. He felt his neck heat up. Why was she looking at Jared like that? Like she wanted to be kissed. And why were they dancing so damn close and laughing like that? His hand tightened on the neck of the bottle he was holding.

Jared whispered in Savannah's ear and Jake could see her blush from here. *That did it!* He slammed the bottle down on the patio table. He *would* kill him. *After* he maimed him. He started to make his way to them, then swore again and stopped himself short.

What was he going to do? Play the wounded husband? He wasn't her husband. He wasn't even her lover. He had no claim on Savannah. She'd said it herself—they wanted different things. Beating up every man who looked at her wasn't going to change that. He could punch out twenty guys and it wouldn't ease the ache he felt for her.

So what was the use? He'd only make a bigger fool out of himself, and Emma probably wouldn't even speak to him. Jaw set tight, Jake did the only other thing he could do.

He headed for the bar.

Seven

"Simon says, touch your nose." Savannah touched her finger to her nose, and all the children, now gathered around her under a tree a short distance from the party, followed suit.

"Simon says, wiggle your ears without using your hands."

The children screwed up their faces and worked furiously to wiggle their ears. Emma, sitting cross-legged on the ground, squinted her eyes and wrinkled her nose. Her new friend, a little blond girl named Amy, furrowed her brow and pursed her lips.

Savannah stood back and laughed, thankful she'd finally managed to escape from the dance floor. After an hour of nonstop two-stepping and twirling, her feet were killing her. She must have danced with every man at the party at least twice, some even three times.

Every man except Jake.

She hadn't even seen him since her dance with Jared, though she'd watched for him. Come to think of it, she hadn't seen that redhead, either, the one who'd stopped him when he'd been walking toward her.

The mellow strain of slow music drifted on the cool evening air, and Savannah glanced at the dance-and-pool area. A full moon shimmered in the water, and the couples held each other close in the flickering lights of patio torches.

As Savannah stared at the dancers, she had a sudden yearning to be in Jake's arms, her body moving with his to the rhythm of the music. If she laid her cheek on his chest, would she hear his heartbeat? If she touched his skin, would it be as hot as it had been when he'd kissed her?

And was he out there now, she wondered, holding that redhead?

A burst of giggles from the little girls brought Savannah out of her wandering thoughts. One of the boys had actually managed to wiggle his ears and the other boys were gathered around him in admiration.

"Spread your arms wide," Savannah said loudly, stretching her arms out from her sides, forcing her attention back to the game. Most of the children copied her, then realized quickly she hadn't said, "Simon says."

Amid the groans and complaints, someone yelled it was time for ice-cream sundaes. Game forgotten, the children ran off, leaving Savannah alone. With a sigh, she leaned back against the tree and listened to the slow country ballad. An ache spread through her as she watched the dancers. Unwillingly she scanned the crowd, hoping to catch a glimpse of one tall cowboy with a black Stetson, praying she wouldn't find him in another woman's arms.

Foolish thoughts, she told herself, but that didn't stop her. Every time he came close, every time he looked at her, she felt the energy pulsate between them. Her heart beat faster and her stomach twisted into a knot. She either needed a doctor or a lover, she thought with a wry smile. But did she

dare let her guard down and give in to the attraction she felt
for Jake? It would be so easy. So very easy—

"A penny for your thoughts."

Startled, Savannah turned. It was Sam. "I was just en-
joying the music," she said, trying to keep the disappointment out of her voice.

"Alone?" He leaned a shoulder on the trunk of the tree
and faced her.

She forced a smile. "I'm afraid my admirers left me in
lieu of ice-cream sundaes."

"Not all your admirers," he said, leaning closer.

The bark of the tree scraped against Savannah's back as
she inched away. "You have a lovely home," she said, ignoring Sam's blatant come-on.

"You never got a chance to accept my invitation to come
out to the ranch one afternoon. We could go to dinner after."

After what? Savannah wanted to ask. "Uh...why don't
I call you?"

He leaned away and looked at her for a long minute.
"Maybe I've misunderstood your relationship with Jake,"
he said carefully. "If I'm stepping in on his—"

Savannah felt her cheeks flame. "You're not stepping in
on anything. I'm here as Emma's aunt and guardian, nothing else." She emphasized "else."

"I see." Sam lifted one eyebrow and smiled. "Well, then,
as Emma's aunt and guardian, are you also handling her
business affairs?"

She didn't like the word "affair" when Sam McCants was
involved. "What business affairs?"

"The land J.T. left Emma," Sam said. "I've tried to talk
to Jake about buying it, but he's managed to avoid the subject every time I bring it up."

Avoidance is Jake's specialty, Savannah thought. "What
about the land?"

"I could use some extra grazing land." He leaned closer to her again. "Maybe we can work out a deal that will satisfy both of us."

"It's not for sale."

Savannah jumped at the sound of Jake's voice. He stood a few feet away, his thumbs shoved tightly in his belt loops, his gaze intense as he stared first at Sam, then at her. A wave of relief washed over her at his timely interruption, but for the life of her, she couldn't understand why she also felt guilty.

"Everything has a price, Jake." Sam smiled and leaned back against the tree. "Name it. Emma could use college money more than grazing land."

"I'm touched you're so concerned about my sister's education," Jake said dryly. "But I'll manage to pay for her college when the time comes."

He'd pay for her college? Savannah started to object, but the men were too busy testing their testosterone levels to pay her any attention.

Sam pushed away from the tree. "Dammit, Jake, if you weren't so bullheaded, you just might see—"

"The only thing I see—" Jake took a step closer to Sam "—is you butting in where you aren't invited. You stick your nose in my business again and you'll be breathing out the back of your head."

Savannah stared at the two men in disbelief. They stood nose to nose, their eyes narrowed and bodies tense. What was going on here? Even though she realized that wars were fought over land, these two looked as if they were ready to kill each other.

She stepped beside Jake and laid a hand on his arm. "Jake," she said tightly, "can we please talk about this later?"

He stared down at her hand. "I'll wait for you and Emma in the truck." He looked back at Sam. "Some things don't have a price tag, Sam. Not for any amount."

His body rigid, Jake turned and walked away. Savannah stared after him, unsure if she should follow and try to talk to him. Right now, though, it might be like trying to talk to a fence post. Clearing her throat, she turned back to Sam and smiled awkwardly. "I—I'm sorry. Emma's land seems to be a sensitive subject with Jake."

Sam shook his head. "That wasn't about Emma's land, Savannah." He leaned back against the tree again and looked at her curiously. "He wasn't even this touchy with Carolyn, his ex."

Carolyn. Jake's ex-wife. Savannah hadn't even known her name. "You knew her?"

He nodded grimly. "I knew her."

It was none of her business, she told herself. Still, a driving need to know more about the woman nagged at Savannah. "Were they married long?"

Sam shrugged. "They probably felt as if they had been, but it was actually only a couple of years. She had a romantic notion of what ranch life was like and he wanted kids. Seems they both lost out."

Jake had said his wife left because of money, but Sam was implying it was more than that. Though tempted to question him further, Savannah knew she had no right. If Jake wanted her to know something, then he'd tell her himself.

Yeah, sure, he would. Just like he'd told her about the land.

She faced Sam and offered her hand. "Thank you for including Emma and me tonight, Sam. We had a nice time."

Sam wrapped his fingers around hers and grinned. "Don't mention it. And if Jake can't get his head out of a dark place, give me a call. I have the feeling it just might be worth Jake rearranging my nose."

He walked away, whistling, and Savannah stared thoughtfully after him. Something told her there was a lot more going on between Sam and Jake than either one of them had let on.

"Aunt Savannah!"

She turned sharply at the sound of Emma's call. Her niece was running across the yard with her friend, Amy.

"Aunt Savannah! Aunt Savannah!" Emma launched herself at Savannah and threw her arms around her waist. "Amy asked me to come to her birthday party tomorrow and Jessica says I can spend the night with her and she'll take me to the party tomorrow. Can I please, please go?"

Off balance, Savannah grabbed hold of her niece so they wouldn't both fall. It took a moment to absorb the child's words.

"I don't know, Pecan. We really can't ask Jessica—"

Jessica walked up then. "It's no problem at all. I'd love for Emma to stay with me. We can shop in the morning for a present and I can bring her home after the party."

"Please, please," both Emma and Amy echoed.

Savannah looked down at the children's pleading faces, then at Jessica. They all stared at her expectantly. How could she say no?

She drew a slow breath and nodded. Emma and Amy screamed and hugged each other, then Emma kissed Savannah goodbye and the girls ran off.

"She'll be fine," Jessica reassured Savannah with a hug, then followed the girls.

Savannah swallowed down the tight feeling in her throat as she watched them walk away. It wasn't Emma she was worried about, Savannah thought. It was herself.

She and Jake were going to be alone.

Jake swung his pickup off the main road and headed for the ranch. Savannah sat beside him, her arms folded stiffly as she stared out the window. The silence between them had been as brittle as dried corn husks. He gripped the steering wheel tighter and floored the accelerator. How did women always do that? he thought angrily. Turn a situation around so the men were the bad guys. Did they learn that in school, or was there some secret ritual where they passed on every annoying habit that drove men crazy from one generation of females to the next?

She grabbed hold of the armrest as he hit a ditch, but still refused to look at him. *Good,* he thought. If he was going to be annoyed, he wanted some company.

He stopped the truck in front of the house and came around to open Savannah's door, but she'd already slid out of the cab herself and brushed past him.

She was also limping.

"What's wrong with you?" He followed her.

She took another step, then winced. "My feet hurt."

A smart reply was on the tip of Jake's tongue, but when Savannah bent over to pull off one of her boots, any intelligible word he might have uttered flew out the window. She obviously had no idea that the view she suddenly offered of her rounded derriere was like a white-hot kick in the gut.

Jaw slack, he stood there, taking in the erotic sight of her. As she pulled off her second boot, her hair spilled over her shoulder, reminding him of wheat fields under a midnight moon. Her long legs were bare, and he followed the slender curve all the way from her toes up to the edge of her short skirt, which skimmed the enticing flesh where thigh met buttocks.

Boots in hand, Savannah straightened and wiggled her toes. She closed her eyes and the soft sigh of contentment that passed between her parted lips had Jake silently cursing. She had to be doing this to him on purpose. She couldn't be so naive that she didn't realize the effect she had on him.

After Jake reminded himself to breathe, he dragged his gaze away from Savannah's legs and moved past her. Teeth set, he held the front door open for her as she walked tentatively up the steps and into the house.

Inside, moonlight washed the living room in pale silver. He watched as Savannah set her boots by the couch, then sank into the cushions with a small groan.

"You should have warned me that Texans like to dance so much. I would have worn slippers, instead of new boots." She closed her eyes and leaned her head back. "I think I know what the term 'bone tired' really means."

He thought about turning on the light, but didn't. Instead, he moved over to the couch and stared down at her. Her lashes were dark against her pale skin, her lips full. He watched the soft rise and fall of her breasts and knew he should leave. Now.

He sat down beside her.

Savannah felt the cushion beside her dip beneath Jake's weight. Cautiously she opened her eyes and stared at him. Considering the mood he'd been in since he'd walked up to her and Sam, she'd expected him to storm off to his room the minute they got inside.

The soft hum of the refrigerator filled the silence, and somewhere a clock was ticking. As she met his dark gaze, the anger drained away and her heart began to pound heavily.

He was close. So incredibly, wonderfully close. The faint smell of sandalwood after-shave drifted to her, mixed with the intoxicating scent of Jake's own masculinity. The combination was exciting, and the curling sensation in her stomach spread through her like warm honey.

When he reached down and pulled her leg across his thigh, she pulled away.

He tugged her gently back. "Relax."

"Jake, I don't—"

"Simon says, relax, Savannah."

A shiver whispered over her skin when he said her name. And she also realized he'd been watching her as she'd played games with the children. Her breath caught as his hand slid over her calf.

This isn't a good idea, she reminded herself, but when his hand moved down to her foot, tingles shot from the tips of her toes to the tips of her fingers. She laid her head back and sighed.

"You danced a lot tonight," he murmured.

But not with you. "What did you do?"

"I was around."

With that redhead? Savannah wondered. "Around where?"

Jake was amazed at how smooth Savannah's skin was. Like rose petals. He moved up to her ankle, then skimmed his palm over her calf. He knew he should stop. But he couldn't. It wasn't humanly possible. And he was feeling extremely and primitively human at the moment.

He wanted to possess this woman. In every way. He wanted her body and her heart and even her soul. He wanted his name on her lips, her body writhing under his. The image of her in any other man's arms, even his own brother's, sent a wave of fury through him. He tightened his hold on her, shifting his weight on the couch, pressing her back against the cushions with his body. Her eyes flew open at the sudden movement.

"I'll tell you where I was, Savannah. I was at the bar, determined to forget about you. Determined that I wouldn't touch you again or dream about you night after night. I thought I could drown the ache that rips me in two every time I look at you, but it didn't take long to realize that nothing was going to ease that pain."

He stared down at her wide eyes, felt her tremble against him. "Nothing except this."

He caught her mouth with his, felt the protest as she surged upward. But when her lips opened to his and her arms came around his neck, he realized there was no protest, only acceptance.

Her surrender aroused him fully, invoking a sense of power in him he'd never before experienced. The velvet stroke of her tongue against his own was as heady as any wine, as electrifying as a bolt of lightning. The small whimper that shuddered from her throat into his nearly sent him over the edge.

He pulled his mouth from hers and dragged a hot trail of kisses down her throat. "Savannah," he said roughly, "you've got to tell me now if you want me to stop. God help me, I won't be able to in three seconds."

Savannah stilled, and the sound of her heart thundered in her head. Three seconds to make a decision that she knew would change the rest of her life. There could be no recriminations later, no excuses that she hadn't been aware of what she was doing. Immediately her mind began to argue with her body. *He'll hurt you, Savannah. He's made it clear he doesn't want commitment. This is purely physical....*

But the feel of his mouth on her neck drove every rational thought from her mind. The time had come to trust her heart, not her head. She wanted him every bit as much as he wanted her. There would be a price to pay, and that was something she would have to accept.

Her hands moved sensuously down his chest toward his belt buckle. "Don't stop," she whispered.

Relief swept over Jake, followed by a wave of desire so strong it frightened him. He hesitated at the thought. Sex had never frightened him before. Not even his first time when he was sixteen. So why now? Why was this different?

Savannah felt Jake's hesitation and she slowly opened her eyes. She saw the uncertainty in his gaze and knew he was wrestling with some inner demon. She also knew that he wanted her; the arousal pressing against her thigh proved that. And she wanted him. More than she ever would have dreamed possible. They would both have to deal with their own demons later, but for now, there was only this moment. No yesterday. No tomorrow. No land. No Emma.

She drew him to her as if he were her next breath, her next heartbeat. "Make love to me, Jake," she whispered against his mouth. "Please."

Savannah's soft plea was Jake's undoing. His control snapped and he went over the edge he'd been desperately clinging to. His lips covered hers again and again, making love to her mouth while his hands slipped down to cup her breasts. Her sharp intake of breath spurred him on and he quickly tugged her blouse from the waist of her skirt. His fingers slid over the warm skin of her stomach then deftly unsnapped the front clasp of her bra. He filled his hands with her soft firm flesh, massaging the hard peaks of her nipples with his thumbs. She moaned into his mouth.

"Savannah," he murmured, his voice raspy, "you're making me crazy."

She wanted to tell him she was just as crazy, but it was impossible to think. And when she felt his lips move down her neck, then lower still, she gave up trying. Deftly he unbuttoned her blouse and pushed the fabric out of the way. Sensation after incredible sensation rippled through her as his mouth closed over the tip of one aching breast. His tongue was hot and moist and she cried out, arching toward him, raking her nails over his shoulders.

He lavished the same attention on her other breast, until she thought her bones might melt from the sheer heat.

Breathing heavily, he dragged himself away from her and stood, reaching down to take her hand. "In the bedroom," he said raggedly. "I . . . have protection in there."

Protection? Her eyes widened as his meaning sank through the fog of pleasure surrounding her. *Dear Lord,* she thought, taking his hand, how could she have forgotten? Embarrassment heated her cheeks and neck. A moment of awkwardness came over her, but he pulled her to him and when his mouth covered hers, she knew this was right, that she was where she belonged.

They moved toward the bedroom slowly, wrapped in each other's arms. He kissed her deeply, again and again, shedding her blouse and bra along the way while she worked at the buttons of his shirt. Savannah slid her hands over Jake's chest and he moaned, stopping in the hallway to press her back against the wall while he slipped her skirt down. Except for her panties, she was naked. His hands cupped her bottom and he lifted her against him, pressing his arousal against the juncture of her thighs.

Their gazes locked in the dim light, and as she slipped her fingers between them and unhooked the button of his jeans, a blaze of passion burst forth in Jake's eyes. The soft rasp of his zipper and the heavy sound of their breathing filled the warm night air. Her fingers slid under the waistband of his jeans.

Jake took hold of Savannah's hand and stopped the path her fingers had taken. "We'll never make it to the bedroom if you do that," he said hoarsely, then lifted her. He stared into her eyes, his gaze narrowed and intense. "Wrap your legs around me."

She did and he moaned, pressing her back against the wall again as he moved his lips over hers. He pulled her tightly to him and carried her to the bedroom, letting her slide down his body as he released her.

"Now, Savannah," he said huskily.

Her heart pounded with an urgency she'd never felt before. Spreading her fingers, she slid her hands down Jake's hard chest, then slid his jeans and briefs downward. His hips were smooth and lean, muscled like a powerful sleek animal. His arousal was powerful, exciting, but she suddenly felt unsure of herself.

Sensing her uncertainty, his hands closed over her wrists, guiding her to him. He whispered her name, encouraging her, and soon she felt the power of her own sexuality. She heard him moan and the response she elicited excited her beyond anything she'd ever experienced. Velvet steel, she thought.

He turned away from her, reaching to the nightstand, and a moment later he wrapped his arms around her and they fell to the bed. His hand slid along the side of her body, over her hip, pulling her panties away.

He entered her in one furious thrust.

Savannah gasped, and a wave of intense pleasure burst inside of her. Closing her eyes, she instinctively lifted her hips. A sound, more animal than human, rumbled from deep in Jake's throat.

"Open your eyes," he said roughly. "Look at me, Savannah."

She did as he asked. She would have done anything he'd asked at that moment. Heat coiled inside her and it felt as if she were tearing apart. He filled her, bringing her to the brink, then pulling away. He moved slowly, holding her gaze with his, holding her hips still when she attempted to hurry him.

"Jake," she breathed, "please . . . I can't . . ."

"Yes, you can," he whispered hoarsely. "I want to watch you go crazy, baby. Just for me." He began to move faster. "Only for me."

Savannah caught her lower lip, but she couldn't stop the moan. Her blood pounded in her temples. Her heart hammered in her chest. And still she held his gaze.

She called him names. A mixture of endearments and cursing. He only smiled, filling her again and again with exquisite deliberateness.

Until she did go crazy.

And to her ultimate satisfaction, she brought him with her.

There was no perception of time for Savannah. Only a dim hazy awareness of the moonlit room and the slow return of the senses. The tick of the bedside clock, the lone call of a night bird. Damp skin against damp skin. The pressure of the soft mattress against her back and a hard muscled body on top of her.

She couldn't move. Jake shifted his weight, pulling her onto her side without breaking the intimate connection of their bodies. She smiled contentedly, amazed he was able to do that. His lips grazed the length of her collarbone and moved slowly up her neck.

She waited for the avalanche of expected emotions to roll over her and carry her away. Embarrassment. Guilt. Regret. Most certainly regret.

Nothing. She felt none of those things. Only an incredible sense of the world being right. That she was where she belonged. Perhaps tomorrow she'd feel differently, but for now, she had an extraordinary desire to purr.

"Remind me to thank Jessica for keeping Emma tonight," Jake said between ragged breaths.

Savannah smiled and ran her fingers down the sinews of Jake's arm. "And Amy."

His teeth nibbled on her earlobe. "Hmm. And Amy's mother."

Her fingers skated across his thigh. "And Amy's fath—"

He caught her mouth with his, cutting off her words. His kiss was possessive, as ardent as it was passionate.

Jake wanted desperately to tell her what he was feeling, but he didn't understand it himself. He'd thought he could distance himself once they made love. That he'd be able to think clearly and logically. But he couldn't. Not yet.

He pulled her against him and marveled at the silky feel of her hair against his shoulder and the soft brush of her breasts against his chest.

Her fingers trailed lazily over his arm. "I thought you'd gone off with a redhead tonight," she admitted.

"Redhead?" Jake's brow knotted. "Oh, you mean Marie."

She looked up at him, but he said nothing else. Savannah frowned and pinched his arm. He laughed and pulled her tighter to him. "Marie is crazy about Jared. Every time she sees me, she asks how he's doing, but what she really wants to know is does she have a chance with him."

So the woman hadn't been after Jake. Savannah smiled against Jake's chest. "Does she?"

Jake let out a long heavy breath and shook his head. "Jared's too busy blaming himself for Jonathan's death to get involved with anyone."

Savannah lifted her head and looked up at Jake. "Jonathan?"

He moved away from her then and sat, leaning back against the headboard. "Jonathan was our brother, Jared's twin. He died three years ago in an oil-rig accident. Jared blames himself."

Jared's twin. Savannah remembered the picture in the hallway with Jared and another boy. It had been Jonathan, she realized now. "I'm sorry," she whispered, then moved into his arms.

"Yeah," he said softly, running his fingers over Savannah's hair. "We all miss him."

Savannah listened as Jake's heart slowly returned to normal. She'd lost a sister, he a brother. They both understood the pain of that loss. When she pressed her lips to Jake's chest, his hands moved down and tightened on her shoulders.

"There's something you still have to do tonight, Savannah," he murmured against her temple.

She pulled away and looked into his eyes. "And what's that?"

"Dance with me."

She raised one brow. "Exactly what kind of dancing did you have in mind?"

One corner of his mouth turned up and his eyes smiled. "Something slow."

She lifted her mouth to his. "I thought you'd never ask."

She raised one eyebrow. "Exactly what kind of dancing did
you have in mind."

"Just this." His mouth turned up and he lowered his head.
"And this." His mouth found hers. "I thought you'd never ask."

Eight

Jake was already gone when Savannah awoke the next
morning. Dawn was barely more than a pale streak across
the horizon. She felt guilty that she'd slept while he worked.

Yet she also felt wonderful.

Savannah arched her back, then sat up, watching the
early-morning light gently nudge the day. The sheets were a
rumpled mess, much as she imagined herself, and the blanket was lying on the floor beside the bed.

Jake's bed.

Closing her eyes, Savannah leaned back against the an-
tique mahogany headboard and sighed. She'd known that
they would make love. She may have denied it on a con-
scious level, but inside, deep down where that little voice
whispered, she'd known all along. Maybe even from the first
time they'd met, when he'd taken her hand in his. Even
then, it had been powerful.

Powerful. That was the word. How else could she de-
scribe what had happened between them? Beautiful, yes.

Incredible, definitely. But "powerful" gave the feeling a life of its own. Lord knew, it certainly had a mind of its own. Her cheeks grew hot as she remembered her unusual—or should she say animated—lack of inhibition. They'd slept, but never for long. It took only a brush of lips, or the slightest touch of a hand, and they were in each other's arms again with an urgency that had shocked them both.

But what really shocked her was that now, as she lay in Jake's bed, she felt no regret. She refused to spoil the most incredible night of her life by wishing it hadn't happened. It *had* happened.

And she was in love.

From the first moment he'd placed his hand in hers she'd been acutely aware of something between them. She'd told herself it was just physical, that it would pass, but in her heart, she'd known all along that it went much deeper than that. It had come to life when he'd kissed her that first time after they'd fallen in the mud hole, and grown with intensity as each day passed. She could no more have prevented it than she could stop the sun from rising.

With a sigh, she stared out the window again. The sun had risen. They'd spent the night together, made love, and now it was just another day. Jake had made it clear he wanted no ties, no commitments. She had no reason to believe he felt any different about that now than he did last night. For him, it had been physical. *She* was the one with the problem.

She frowned. Falling in love with Jake was going to make her life extremely complicated. But then, when it came to Jake, what else could she expect?

Jake pitched the last of the hay into the end stall, then shut off the water spigot filling the trough. Rosemary moved closer and nudged Jake's pocket. Savannah had been riding the chestnut mare almost every day, and the animal had come to expect a treat.

"Savannah's been spoiling you, hasn't she?" he said, and pulled out a hunk of carrot. Rosemary snatched it up and crunched loudly. "Better not get used to it," Jake warned the mare as he rubbed her ears.

Listen to your own advice, he told himself as he closed the stall gate. After last night, it would be so easy to let himself get used to a lot of things. *Like the feel of warm, soft skin against his every night. The touch of silky hair against his chest. Someone to whisper thoughts to in the early morning....*

Not just any someone. Savannah.

She'd gotten to him. More than he wanted to admit. More than he'd ever dreamed possible. And there wasn't a damn thing he could do about it.

Was there?

No. He'd been down that road before. City women couldn't cut it here for the long term. Carolyn had been all right the first six months. Then she'd started traveling with Myrna to "visit civilization." Then she'd started traveling on her own. He hadn't the money or the patience to support that then. And he sure as hell didn't have it now.

You think I'd raise kids in this hayseed town? Not in a million years, cowboy.

Emma's calf bawled at him from the corner stall, waiting impatiently for her breakfast. Jake realized he'd clenched his hands into fists, and he loosened his fingers, letting the anger pass through him. There were some things a man never forgave.

He picked up one of the bottles of formula he'd brought with him from the house. "You miss Emma, don't you, Betsy?" Jake crooned, heading for the stall. "I guess I do, too."

He did miss her. She'd been gone one day and he found himself anxious for her return. Not that he'd have missed last night for anything, he thought with a slow smile. In fact, if he hurried, maybe he could get back before Savannah awoke. He was tired, but he wasn't *that* tired.

She'd been sleeping peacefully when he'd slipped out of bed this morning. He'd had the most incredible urge to pull her in his arms and just hold her, nothing else. Just hold her and tell her—

Tell her what?

"Good morning."

He spun abruptly at the sound of her soft voice. She was dressed already, in jeans and a blue shirt rolled to the elbows. Her hair fell loosely around her shoulders. As her gaze met his, he realized there were faint shadows under her eyes. Her cheeks were cranberry red.

She was embarrassed, he realized.

He set the bottle down and walked toward her. When he pulled her into his arms and kissed her, she came willingly. Eagerly. *Thank God,* he thought.

"It is now," he whispered against her cheek, then kissed her again. Deeply.

She responded to his kiss by slipping her arms around his neck and pressing her body against his.

"I can't get enough of you," he murmured, moving her toward a pile of fresh hay.

She laughed softly. "You certainly are trying."

Arms entwined, they fell together on the hay. He kissed her, and her lips were warm and pliant under his. She was so soft, he thought, so incredibly soft. He rolled her onto her back and reached for the snap of her jeans. Her eyes glinted with passion and she reached for him, as well.

Betsy bawled again.

Jake sighed and laid his forehead against Savannah's. "That cow is going to be steaks before this day is through."

Savannah rose reluctantly and brushed the hay off her jeans. "Don't let Emma hear you say that. She's got Betsy entered in the Roundup next week."

Picking up the bottle, Savannah moved toward the calf. Betsy clamped down hungrily on the nipple. Jake watched her feed the animal and a strange feeling centered itself in his chest. In the two years his ex-wife had been here, she'd never once come near any of the animals. She'd hated the smell and the dirt.

"Savannah." He moved beside her.

She smoothed the hair between Betsy's ears. "Hmm?"

His heart began to pound and his palms felt sweaty. "I want you to stay."

Her hand stilled, but she didn't look at him. "Stay?"

"Here," he said. "With me. You and Emma."

She stared at Betsy. "I'm not sure what you mean."

Dammit, why was she making this so difficult? Did she have any idea how hard this was for him? "I want you and Emma to come live here, at Stone Creek."

She set the nearly empty bottle down and rose slowly. Her gaze lifted to him and he saw the cautious look in her eyes. "In what capacity?"

In what capacity? It wasn't as if he was hiring, for God's sake. "You and me, and Emma."

Her lips thinned. "Why?"

He felt his jaw tense. "We're good together, Savannah. Last night proved that. And as far as Emma is concerned, a family would be good for her."

Savannah stared at him for a long moment. "That's right, Jake," she said with deadly calm. "A family would be good for Emma. A *real* family. If you're looking for a live-in, no-strings-attached bedmate, try the Help Wanted section of the newspaper."

"Savannah, just listen—"

She cut him off with a wave of her hand. "Have you given any consideration to Emma and the kind of example we'd be setting for her if we lived here under those conditions?"

"People live together all the time. It's a fact of life."

"It's not a fact of *my* life, Jake. And it's not going to be for Emma, either. My sister may have fallen in love with the wrong man and gotten pregnant, but I have no intention of making that same mistake."

Jake felt as if a fist had punched him in the stomach. His eyes narrowed. "Are you saying that having a baby with me would be a mistake?"

She closed her eyes and drew a deep breath. "You haven't heard one word I've said, have you?" she said quietly.

When she opened her eyes again, he saw the hurt there. He just didn't understand it. "The answer is no, Jake. I won't live with you, not like that."

Shoulders stiff, head high, she walked past him and out of the barn.

Fine, then. He clenched and unclenched his hands, resisting the urge to follow her. Let her walk. Better now than later. If she didn't care enough to stay and give it a try, then he'd completely misunderstood last night. It wasn't the first time he'd been wrong about a woman.

But he sure as hell intended to see that it would be the last.

Stone Manor was an opulent, twenty-three-room mansion that sat dead center in the one hundred thousand acres that made up Stone Creek. The exterior of the house was something on the order of Georgian Colonial, while the interior ran somewhere along the lines of Greek Revival. In the entry, Emma stared openmouthed at a marble fountain surrounded by alabaster water maidens, then made faces at herself in the glossy white marble floors. Green silk covered the walls, and gold trimmed the extensive thick moldings.

It was the most elaborate, ornately decorated home that Savannah had ever seen. And the fact that it was in the middle of nowhere made it all the more confusing. Savannah was beginning to understand a little more clearly Jake's hostility toward this woman. He worked fourteen-hour days with almost no help just to keep the ranch operating, while Myrna had spent thousands of dollars on wall murals of fat-cheeked cherubs.

Savannah had tried to get out of the lunch date with Jake's stepmother, but after canceling twice using flimsy excuses, there was no avoiding it. Myrna had just completed a grand tour of the mansion, with all twenty-three rooms described in excruciating detail, then left Savannah and Emma in the parlor while she saw about lunch. Emma sat on the edge of the cream damask couch beside Savannah, swinging her feet and toying with the blue buttons on the front of her paisley jumper.

"Aunt Savannah, when can we go home?"

"Soon, sweetie. After we eat lunch."

"I need to feed Betsy." Emma's voice was close to a whine. Savannah didn't blame her. A whine seemed quite appropriate after an hour with Myrna.

The woman came through a pair of double doors at that moment, carrying a silver tray. She bent down in front of Emma and held the tray toward her. "Try a bite of the veal pâté, dear. It's really quite tasty."

The child eyed the molded brownish concoction with serious misgivings, then glanced up at Savannah. "What's veal pâté?"

Savannah shifted uncomfortably. "It's, uh, well . . ."

Myrna set the tray down. "It's calf's liver, dear. It's very tender if the calf is young."

"Calf's liver?" Emma stared at Myrna in horror. "You mean, like Betsy?"

Myrna frowned. "Betsy?"

Savannah straightened quickly. "Emma, would you please go get my purse? I left it on the table by the front door."

Thankful for any excuse to escape, Emma jumped up. "Can I play with the fish in the fountain?"

"Just watch them." Savannah breathed a sigh of relief as Emma left the room. That had been a little too close.

Myrna stared after the child, her brow furrowed. "I'm afraid I've never been around children very much. I was an only child and my mother left when I was ten. Daddy has always taken care of me, given me everything I've wanted. I can't help wondering what it would have been like if J.T. and I had ... well, if we'd had a child."

"Maybe we shouldn't have come," Savannah said carefully and started to rise.

"No, no." Myrna waved her back. "Please don't go. I'm sorry if I've made you uncomfortable, but I need to talk to you. About Emma's land."

Savannah had wondered when she'd get around to the subject. "What about it?"

"I'm interested in buying it, and I'd like to know what your intentions are."

Her only intentions at this moment were to get this lunch over with as soon as possible. "I haven't any."

"Jake's executor of the estate, you know." Myrna took a bite of the cracker. "He'll fight you if you decide to sell."

A familiar pain tightened around Savannah's heart. She and Jake had barely spoken since that morning in the barn after the night they'd made love. That had been three days ago. Three long agonizing days. And nights. The nights had been even longer. In one weak desperate moment she'd even considered accepting his offer to live with him. The thought of living without him was unbearable.

But she couldn't. There was more to love than the physical. There was respect and honor and trust. Jake obviously felt none of those things for her, and she knew she'd certainly never respect herself if she gave in. And while self-respect might not keep her warm on a cold night, at least she'd be able to look at herself in the mirror every morning.

"As Emma's guardian, I believe I have the final say what happens to the land," Savannah said firmly.

"But what if you weren't her guardian?" Myrna asked. "The Stone children can be very persuasive. A court might grant custody to a brother or sister over an aunt."

She didn't believe they would do that. She *couldn't* believe it. Still, cold dread formed in the pit of her stomach. "There's been no indication they might do that," Savannah said hesitantly.

"There was no indication before Jake served his wife with divorce papers, either," Myrna said with a knowing lift of her brow. "He tossed that woman out like a sack of trash just because she wanted a few nice things. He won't give you the advantage of a warning. He's a cold man, Savannah. Be careful of him. He'll do whatever it takes to get what he wants."

Would he? Savannah stared at the pâté and a sick feeling overwhelmed her. She couldn't believe that. She *wouldn't* believe it.

"How interesting," Savannah said coolly, but she refused to let Myrna know she'd gotten to her. "Jake said the same thing about you."

Savannah was curled up on the living room couch when Jake came in the back door that night. It was after nine. She heard the refrigerator door open, then the pop of a soda can. She lowered the mystery novel she'd been attempting to read for the past hour. Somehow she'd managed to get through a chapter, but couldn't remember one word she'd read.

Her heart began to pound as she set the book aside and unfolded herself from the couch. She had to face him sometime. They couldn't keep avoiding each other like this. Sooner or later, they were going to have to talk, if not for their own sakes, then for Emma's.

Drawing a steadying breath, she walked barefoot to the kitchen door and pulled her robe tightly around her as she stood there and watched him moving things around inside the refrigerator. He hadn't turned the overhead light on, but the lamp inside the refrigerator illuminated the room and silhouetted his long muscular frame as he bent over and stared at the food. His jeans were covered with mud, and she noticed he was in his stocking feet.

She felt a stab of sympathy, knowing he'd been out since dawn. She considered postponing the talk she wanted to have with him, but it couldn't wait. She had to know.

"There's a plate of chicken on the top shelf," she said quietly.

He glanced at her over his shoulder. "Thanks."

She watched as he grabbed the plate, then closed the door. The room was dark now, except for the soft glow of the stove light, and he stood there, watching her. Waiting.

How strange, she thought. Three days ago she'd spent the night with this man, made love to him. Now they were like two strangers. She folded her arms tightly, forcing back the pain that sliced through her. "You've had a long day," she said awkwardly.

He moved to the table and sat. "The fence was down again between Sam's and my place, and I had a pump fail at one of the watering stations. I had to run the water manually."

She made her way across the room, wondering why neither one of them had turned on the light. "Emma and I had lunch with Myrna today."

He gave a snort and bit into a chicken leg. "I'd take my day over yours anytime."

At least he still had some sense of humor left, even if it was sarcasm. "Jake, I need to talk to you."

His shoulders stiffened for a fraction of a second, then he reached for his soda and took a long drink. He wiped his mouth with the back of his hand and stared at her. "So talk."

Savannah sighed and sat in the chair opposite him. "It's just that, well, Emma—"

He started to rise out of his seat. "So help me, if that woman said one word to Emma, I'll—"

"No." She shook her head. "That's not what I'm trying to say."

He settled back down in his seat, but his dark gaze locked with hers. "It's been a long day and I'm tired. Myrna's the last subject I care to discuss. Just say it, Savannah."

She drew a deep breath. "Do you have any intention of obtaining custody of Emma?"

His eyes narrowed. "What?"

She could see the anger building in him, but it didn't matter. She had to hear him say it. She needed him to look her in the eyes and tell her Myrna was wrong. "I have to know, Jake. Would you try and take Emma away from me?"

He leaned back in his chair and looked at her. "What judge would give a single man, living this far out, custody of a nine-year-old girl?"

He hadn't answered her question, only asked one of his own. "That situation could change at any moment."

"Highly unlikely," he said dryly, then added, "But I suppose you never really know about tomorrow, do you? There might be a woman or two who might not mind living out here."

She winced under the sharp sting of his words. She knew that there were plenty of women who wouldn't mind living with him under his conditions and that he could easily find someone to fill the job. She just hadn't realized he'd be so cruel as to throw it in her face.

Damn. Why hadn't she waited to have this conversation? Waited until she wasn't feeling so open, so vulnerable?

She started to rise, intending to put as much distance between her and Jake as possible, but his hand snaked out and pulled her back. He let out a long heavy sigh. "I'm sorry," he said quietly. "Sit down."

She sat stiffly, but said nothing, just stared at him with her chin held high.

"Tell me exactly what Myrna said," he asked. When she looked away from him, he added, "Please."

She looked down at his hand wrapped around her wrist. His palm was dry and rough, and the texture against her own smooth skin sent shivers up her spine. "That you would have control over Emma's land if she was in your custody. You wouldn't have to worry about it being sold."

"I suppose she told you that right after she offered to buy it?"

Savannah nodded.

"Right." He pulled her closer to him. "What else did she say?"

"She said I should be careful of you. That you'd served your ex-wife divorce papers without warning, and you'd serve Emma's custody papers to me the same way."

Jake's fingers tightened around Savannah's wrist. He was looking at her, but she had the distinct feeling he wasn't seeing her, that he was somewhere else, *with* someone else.

"Jake," she gasped when his grip became unbearable.

He blinked, then quickly released her. Pushing himself away from the table, he stood and stared down at her. "I'm sorry you still don't trust me," he said quietly, then walked out of the room.

Her heart ached as she watched him go.

Nine

Cactus Flat Roundup had been a tradition in the town for the past sixty-two years, ever since local rancher Levi Harper, a New York City immigrant, offered to pay fifty dollars for "the best danged bull in the county." The tradition not only broke up the long hot monotony of the summer, it also provided the contestants in everything from the "best danged rooster" to the "best danged apple pie" with a little extra cash.

And a little extra cash was something Jake was sorely in need of.

He tried not to think about that now as he watched the younger residents of Cactus Flat County parade their entries in the calf competition. There were at least twelve participants, and Emma marched proudly around the covered arena, a determined glint in her blue eyes and a confident swing in her ponytail as she tugged a reluctant Betsy behind her.

She was a Stone, all right, he thought with a grin.

As she passed by him, smiling broadly, Jake also tried not to think about the water pump that had failed and was going to cost twelve hundred dollars to replace. Or the two truck tires that had gone flat the day before yesterday. Tires that were only one year old.

If he didn't know better, he'd swear that someone was intentionally sabotaging him.

Myrna, perhaps? She'd never pulled any punches about wanting his land. Maybe she thought that by systematically wearing him down financially, she might succeed. And the way things were going, she just might be right.

He nearly laughed at the thought. Even Myrna wouldn't stoop that low.

There was Sam, too. He'd been wanting to expand his ranch for years and had offered to buy Stone Creek after J.T. had died. He'd have a lot to gain.

Jake pressed his lips tightly together. No. No matter what had passed between Sam and himself, he still didn't believe that the man was responsible for any of the problems at the ranch.

Damn. He shook his head and rubbed a hand over his face. He was getting downright paranoid. It was bad luck, that was all. Something he seemed to have a nasty case of lately.

Especially when it came to Savannah, he thought grimly, tipping his hat away from his face as he watched her make her way toward him from the other side of the arena.

She was smiling as she approached, something he hadn't seen her do for several days—not since the morning after they'd made love. Her green eyes were bright with excitement, her cheeks flushed with delight. He felt a sharp stab of pleasure, then a longing so intense his breath caught like chickweed in his throat. When she moved beside him, he caught the faint scent of peaches. It took a will of iron to stop himself from pulling her against him and kissing her senseless.

"So what do you think?" she said breathlessly. "Do we have a chance?"

Her words stopped him cold. Then he realized she was talking about Emma and Betsy. He tore his gaze away from Savannah and glanced over at his sister and the calf, lined up for inspection in front of the judges. "There's always a chance."

Savannah moved closer to Jake, making room for a spectator beside her. The short sleeve of her white blouse brushed against his denim shirt, and the simple meeting of fabric between them had his heart pounding as if the contact were bare skin. Beads of sweat formed on his forehead, and he reached up to swipe them away, thankful to break the connection of their clothing.

"She's going to be terribly disappointed if they don't win," Savannah said, oblivious to his discomfort. "Do you think you could say something to cheer her up if necessary?"

Disappointments were a fact of life, he thought soberly, then felt like kicking himself for being a complete idiot. Emma had already had more than her share of disappointment. He nodded stiffly, but he hadn't a clue what he would say. "Sure."

The judges, two elderly gentlemen in identical gray suits, whom Jake knew as the Simpson twins, stood in front of the children and called for everyone's attention. The crowd went quiet and all the children, wide-eyed, stood stock-still. Savannah laid her hand on Jake's arm and squeezed. Her touch distracted him for a moment, but as the names were being called out, he forced his attention to the center of the arena.

Second and first runners-up were named. Neither one was Betsy.

"And the first-place blue ribbon goes to..."

The judge paused dramatically. Jake held his breath. Savannah's fingers tightened on his arm and instinctively he covered her hand with his.

"Emma Roberts and Betsy of Stone Creek Ranch."

With a shriek of delight, Savannah threw her arms around Jake. He laughed and hugged her, then whistled his congratulations to Emma, who was smiling as she hugged Betsy. Jessica and Jared cheered from across the arena.

"That's my little sister," Jake said to a man standing next to him. The man nodded appreciatively, and when Jake looked back at Savannah, the smile on her face had him tightening his arm around her.

Strange how right it felt to share even the smallest joy with her. How easy and how good. And when she lifted her gaze to his, he drew her closer to him. He smiled slowly, and her eyes turned smoky green as he dropped his gaze to her mouth. Her lips parted and she leaned into him—

"Jake! Aunt Savannah!" Emma called and waved to them. "Come look at Betsy's ribbon!"

Sighing silently, Jake pulled away. Savannah smiled at him, and he shook his head as he took her hand and led her across the arena. Jared and Jessica had already congratulated Emma, who stood ramrod straight beside Betsy as their picture was taken for the *Cactus Flat Gazette*.

The crowd was beginning to disperse when a barrelchested cowboy in dusty black boots and worn hat approached Jake. "You Jake Stone?" the man asked.

Jake nodded.

"Carl Potter. Bar M." They shook hands. "You got a minute?"

"Sure." Jake reluctantly let go of Savannah's hand. "I'll be right back."

Savannah watched Jake leave, her senses still on overload from being in his arms. He'd almost kissed her, and her heart was still beating double-time from the anticipation. Her head told her she was a fool because she'd wanted him to, but her heart told her head to shut up.

Jessica and Jared led Betsy back to her pen while Emma ran off to show Amy her blue ribbon. Smiling, Savannah found a quiet place in the now deserted stands and sat to wait—more anxiously than she cared to admit—for Jake to return.

She and Emma would be leaving in a week. Seven days to be exact. She tried to tell herself that once she and her niece were home and school started, they'd both be fine. Life would settle down and they'd get on with their lives, even without Jake. She knew she was doing the right thing, not only for herself, but for Emma.

So why didn't that ease the pain in her heart?

"I seen the youngun' got her blue ribbon."

Savannah jumped at the sound of the gravelly voice behind her. It was Digger. She smiled at him. "She's already run off to show her friends."

The wooden bench bowed beneath the large man's weight as he sat beside her. "Her pa would've been proud of her," he said quietly. "And Miss Angie, too."

Angie? Did he mean Angela? Surprised, Savannah looked at the man. "Did you know my sister, Mr. Montgomery?"

"I'm not much on formalities, Savannah. Digger'll do." He tipped back his hat and placed his hands on the worn knees of his jeans. "Yes, ma'am. I knew your sister. She used to eat at my place when she was living here in town. J.T. and her used to sit at the corner table and go over the blueprints for Myrna's house."

"Digger, how—" Savannah stopped herself, then looked away, watching a small dust devil kick up the dirt as it danced over the arena. It wasn't an easy thing, asking a near stranger about her sister's love affair with a married man. When she turned back, Digger was watching her, his gray eyes soft.

"You can't stand between the raindrops when a thunderstorm hits," he said gently. "Some folks might try, but they get wet, anyway."

He'd understood exactly what she'd been thinking, Savannah realized with relief. And she understood his analogy perfectly. She'd fought her attraction to Jake since day one, and it hadn't done one bit of good. She'd still fallen in love. Hopelessly and completely. Just as Angela had.

Savannah stared at Digger's hands. His fingers were long and weathered, his knuckles swollen from years of work. He was an honest man. A good man. One who made no judgments about his friends. Instinctively she liked him.

The distant sound of a loudspeaker announced that the ladies' baked-goods competition had begun, and the smell of apple pies permeated the hot afternoon air. It was a simple way of life here. One she knew she could get used to. She already had. And the idea of leaving created an empty hollow ache inside her.

She looked back at Digger. There was one question she had to ask. She had to know the answer. "Was J.T., I mean...did he..."

"He loved her." Digger nodded firmly. "There're some things a man's eyes tell that he might never say, but he just about went crazy after she disappeared. If he'd known she was carrying his little one, nothing in the world would have stopped him from finding her."

"You mean, he didn't know?"

Digger shook his head. "He was a bitter man from the day your sister left. After nine years he decided he had to know the truth and he hired that P.I. fellow to find her. That's when he found out about the baby."

He hadn't known about Angela's being pregnant. Relief poured through Savannah.

"It was the first spark of life I'd seen in him since she'd left." Digger covered Savannah's hand with his and she was amazed at how gentle his touch was. "Neither one of them planned what happened, Savannah. He loved your sister more'n life itself, that same kind of love he had for Jake's mama. He was a lucky man to have that twice in his life. Some folks don't even find it once."

I've found it, Savannah thought with an ache in her chest. And she wasn't able to do anything more about it than her sister had.

"Aunt Savannah!"

Savannah jumped up at the sound of Emma's sob. She was running across the arena, her face streaked with tears. Frowning, Digger stood as Savannah ran out to her niece.

"Emma, what's the matter?"

"Amy's brother... Betsy... gone..."

Emma was crying so hard Savannah couldn't understand her.

Jake came running toward them then, his face a tight knot of worry.

"What's wrong?" He knelt beside Emma.

"Jake." Emma threw her arms around him. "Keith, Amy's brother, said that the blue-ribbon cows get sold to be killed and eaten and I told him he was a liar, but Betsy is gone and I can't find her. It's not true, is it? No one's going to kill Betsy and make patty out of her, are they?"

Savannah watched the helpless expression that crossed Jake's face and felt a sense of horror. It *was* true. She could tell by the look in his eyes. *Oh, God.* She hadn't realized. That was where Jake had gone—to sell Betsy. He was a rancher. That was his business. And she knew how desperately he needed the money.

"Emma," Savannah said gently. "Come here, Pecan. We need to talk."

"I don't want to talk!" Emma shoved Jake away. "I want Betsy!"

She ran back toward the holding pens, and Savannah saw the stricken look on Jake's face as he watched her go. She touched his arm and he turned to look at her. The pain in his eyes cut into her heart.

"I've already made the deal and he took the calf," he said helplessly. "I never thought... It never dawned on me—"

"I'll talk to her, Jake. She'll be fine."

"She'll hate me," he said quietly.

"No. She'll get over it."

His single swear word was earthy and to the point. Jaw tight, he walked stiffly away.

Savannah watched him go. She had no idea what she was going to say to Emma. With a weary sigh, she turned and went to find her niece.

The moon was no more than a slice of silver late that night. One wispy cloud hung beneath the brilliant crescent like a filmy garment on a closet hook, and stars, more than anyone could count, lit the midnight blue sky.

It never ceased to amaze Savannah how beautiful it was here. She stood at Emma's open bedroom window, staring out into the darkness. It was quieter out here, calmer. Certainly less complicated than the city.

Less complicated, that was, if you didn't count her falling in love with Jake and Emma's losing Betsy.

Emma had refused to talk to Jake on the ride home from town and had run to her room the minute they'd pulled up at the ranch house. Jake had knocked on her door once, but Emma told him to go away. And he had. He'd gotten back in the truck and torn off, spewing dirt and rocks with his back tires. It was almost eleven o'clock and he still hadn't come back.

With a sigh Savannah turned and crossed to Emma's bed. Her niece had cried herself to sleep, and even now her slumber was troubled. Savannah had told Jake that Emma would get over it, but he hadn't believed her any more than she'd believed it when she'd told herself she'd get over Jake.

A quiet knock at the door startled her. It opened slowly.

"Emma" came a quiet whisper. "Are you awake?"

It was Jake. Thank God. Relief swept through her. The way he'd left here, she'd worried that he was lying half-drunk in a ditch somewhere. She moved toward him, a finger to her lips. "She's sleeping."

"Wake her up."

"She just got—"

At the sound of a bell ringing, Savannah stopped. She realized that Jake had a rope in his hand. He swung the door open wide.

Betsy!

Savannah's hand flew to her mouth and she smothered a gasp. The calf, obviously tired from its busy day, stood in the hall, head drooping, but no worse for wear. Savannah looked sharply at Jake. "But...how? Where...?"

"Betsy!"

Emma's cry of delight shattered the quiet. She flew across the room and wrapped her arms around the calf, hugging the poor animal until it grunted with annoyance.

Through the moisture in her eyes, Savannah looked at Jake. He stood back, hands in his pockets, a grin on his face as he watched Emma. She knew he'd done this for his sister at tremendous cost to himself and the ranch. She wanted to speak, but the emotion swelled in her throat and words were impossible.

"Emma," Jake said softly as he moved closer to her, "I've got to put Betsy in the barn now."

Emma let go of the calf and flung herself into Jake's arms. "You saved her," she said, her voice breaking. "Thank you."

He knelt, hugging her back, then cleared his throat and stood. "Get some sleep. You're going to need to get up early and feed that calf."

Emma nodded eagerly and jumped into her bed, crawling under the covers with a giggle. Jake's gaze met Savannah's for a heart-stopping second, then he picked up the calf and left.

"Jake is the best brother in the whole world," Emma said proudly.

Savannah smiled and smoothed Emma's hair away from her face. "Yes, he is."

"Aunt Savannah, can we come live here with Jake?"

Savannah felt as if her heart had leapt up into her throat. She shook her head. "No, sweetheart, we can't."

"Why not?"

Why not? Such a simple question. Such a difficult answer. "Lots of reasons. We have our own home, for one.

You have school, for another, and I have to get back to work."

"You could get a job at Amy's school. She says it's really neat. They have lots of animals everyone takes care of and she gets to ride the bus every day. They don't have to wear stupid uniforms, either."

St. Mary's Academy *was* rigid, Savannah realized. Not to mention snobbish. Maybe she would look into a new school when they got back. It would be easy enough to find another job. And besides, maybe a change for both of them would be good. A fresh start. Anything that might ease the pain of leaving Stone Creek.

"Let's talk about it tomorrow." Savannah tucked the covers around Emma. "Right now, I want to see those eyes close."

Savannah made her way to the barn in the darkness. The raucous sound of crickets crowded the hot night air, and the distant howl of a coyote reminded her of the isolation here. Strange how the same isolation that once frightened her, now comforted.

Inside the barn, a single light burned, and she heard the rustle of hay as Jake tossed a handful into the end stall. Betsy was lying in the corner, her huge brown eyes drooping soulfully.

"You bought her back from that man, didn't you?" Savannah asked.

Jake brushed his hands off against his jeans, then shut the gate. "Not exactly. I just tore up the check."

Savannah leaned against the stall, watching Jake as he secured the latch. There were dark circles under his eyes and exhaustion had formed creases beside his mouth. "You needed that money for the pump, Jake."

He stared at the sleeping calf. "Do you think I'd let Emma leave here thinking me a murderer?"

"She has to understand sometime what it is you do here. I don't think she's ever really put it together."

"That reminds me." He frowned. "What in the world was that comment Emma made about Betsy and patty?"

Savannah rolled her eyes. "Myrna offered Emma some pâté when we went for lunch the other day, and Emma asked what it was."

Jake shook his head in disgust. "I swear, Betsy has more brains than that woman."

Savannah smiled, then, without thinking, she reached out and touched his arm. "Jake, let me loan you the money for the pump. I have a little put aside for—"

"No."

"It's taking you extra time every day to run that water manually. You're already working yourself into an early grave with the hours you put in. Let me—"

His expression hardened. "I said no."

She'd already known what his response would be, but she'd had to at least try. She dropped her hand away and sighed. "What are you going to do, then?"

He shrugged. "I'll manage."

"I expect you will," she said softly.

His dark gaze locked with hers and when he moved closer, she felt her heart begin to pound. A low steady beat at first, then harder, until it felt as if a fist was hammering in her chest.

"I'd manage a lot better if you'd stay here, Savannah."

His voice was husky, the timbre as seductive as it was exciting. Lord, how she wanted to say yes. *Yes.* Even Emma wanted to stay. It would be so easy....

She closed her eyes and felt the heat of his body as he leaned still nearer. His smell was completely masculine, and she responded at a level where she had no control. He cupped her chin in his hand gently and ran his thumb over her jaw.

"Jake..." She sighed, opening her eyes. She lost whatever it was she wanted to say. His face was so close she could feel his breath on her cheek and see the intricate web of lines at the corners of his eyes. His thumbs moved down her neck with feather softness, promising pleasure she knew only he could give her.

"I've never felt about anyone what I feel for you," he whispered. "Stay with me tonight." His lips brushed hers. "Every night."

Her body was screaming at her to say yes. She leaned into him, parting her lips breathlessly as his hands slid over her shoulders and down her arms.

Could she have him for this one night? Or even a dozen nights? It wouldn't be enough. Just having this part of him would never be enough. She loved him too much. She'd spend the rest of her life aching for a man who could never truly give himself to her. She'd seen what that had done to Angela, and Savannah couldn't bear that. She might never love again as she loved Jake, but she would marry and she would have children. That would have to be enough.

Her hand felt as if it were made of lead as she reached up and laid her fingers on his chest. Gently she pushed him away.

"I can't, Jake," she said softly, turning her head away.

He drew in a deep weary breath and backed away. There was no anger between them this time, just a yearning so strong it drained them both.

"I have a few things to do here," he said, turning away. "You go on and I'll close up the house when I come in."

Hugging her arms to her, Savannah nodded. There wasn't one step all the way back to the house that she didn't curse herself for wanting more than Jake had to give.

Ten

Lightning streaked jaggedly across the west Texas horizon. Dark, heavy-bottomed clouds billowed in, replacing sky that had been deep blue only minutes before. Frowning, Jake stared at the spectacular display, as much in awe of the magnificence of nature as he was annoyed by the unpredictability. There was only one sure thing about the weather in Texas: you could never be sure.

Sort of like a woman, he thought sourly. At least, one particular woman, who plagued his thoughts and haunted his dreams.

Savannah.

Even her name drew the most erotic images to his mind: her incredible silky blond hair flowing over his hot skin, her soft seductive smile as she pressed her lips to his, her slender smooth fingers moving over his body...

Jake shifted in his saddle, cursing his thoughts. Thoughts that would lead nowhere but to a cold shower and a big empty bed. She was leaving in three days. Taking Emma and going back to Atlanta. It was better this way, he told himself. If she stayed, she'd work her way under his skin so deeply, he'd never want her to go. And those feelings were more dangerous than the storm brewing overhead.

Thunder rolled, and Jake's horse, Saucy, tossed her head nervously. No creature, man or otherwise, wanted to be out in a Texas storm. Jake was no exception. He pulled the mare around, intending to head back to the ranch, when he heard the agitated bawling of cows. It was coming from a ravine a short distance away. He spurred his horse toward the sound.

About a dozen steers were trapped at the bottom of the dry riverbed. How the hell they'd managed to break off from the rest of the herd and wind up here, he hadn't a clue, but he knew if he left them here, they'd be dead. If the storm didn't get them, then wolves most certainly would.

With a heavy sigh, Jake eased his horse down the steep ravine. He just wanted to get this done and get back to the ranch. Quickly.

"Easy, Saucy," he crooned to his horse as she resisted the incline. "Take it slow, baby. That's a girl."

Halfway down, lightning flashed again, this time no more than a quarter mile away. Saucy reared, then stumbled, tossing Jake straight over her head. His hat flew off as he landed on the hard ground with a grunt. Before he could even pick himself up, the mare had scrambled back up the embankment.

Dammit! He rose slowly and snatched his hat off a scrubby bush. He'd had enough of skittish females to last him a lifetime, he thought irritably, brushing himself off. Thunder shook the ground again. The first drop struck him on the cheek; the second, on his nose.

Then, as if someone had flipped on a rain switch, the sky opened up.

"Hiiyah!" Jake yelled, running at the cows. Frightened, they broke to the left. Lightning and thunder was simultaneous; rain pounded the dry earth, running off before it had a chance to soak in. His visibility was poor, but Jake waved his arms, hollering behind the terrified animals as he chased them back up the steep ravine.

It took three more attempts before the last cow managed to clear the incline. Drenched to the bone, furious as hell, Jake waded through the already ankle-high water. Mud sucked at his boots, while the increasing current pulled at his legs. He had to get out of here, and fast. Flash floods had surprised more than one unwary rancher, and once a current that strong got hold of a person, it could be miles before his body was found.

Determined not to bring that thought to reality, Jake made his way to the incline. It was like walking through thick molasses. He slipped twice, and each time the soggy earth under his boots tried to drag him down. The third time he lost ground, his hat flew off and floated away like a raft over the rapids. Cursing fluently, Jake righted himself and inched his way to the embankment.

The current was to his knees now, but the rain was coming down so hard and he was so drenched that it was difficult to tell where the water level started or stopped. He slipped again and went under this time, the current sucking him down as if he were a straw doll, instead of a 220-pound man.

All Jake could see was black. Rocks and floating debris pelted his face, and a hollow rushing sound, like the underside of a waterfall, filled his ears. He lost control completely and tumbled several times, the current tossing him like a broken stick.

Gasping for air, he came back up and desperately tried to gain a hold in the doughy ground. His boot hit a rock and he managed to right himself. The embankment was in front of him; all he had to do was get up it. He reached up, but his hands only sank into the sodden earth and came away with fistfuls of mud. A brilliant streak of lightning flashed overhead, illuminating the water and ground in vivid detail.

Two feet away, Jake saw a tree root protruding from the ravine wall. The current attempted to pull him the opposite direction, but he lunged for the root and grabbed hold. Relief poured through him. Once he could pull himself out of the water, he knew he could make it up the incline. He lost his footing twice, but finally managed to drag himself from the raging waters. Muddy or not, Jake vowed, he was going to kiss the ground when he climbed out.

He was nearly to the top when a loud rumble over his head caused him to look up. Rain battered his face and the earth began to shake. The single swear word he'd attempted was cut short as mud and rocks broke loose directly above him and crashed down.

Savannah stood at the living room window, chewing on a ragged fingernail as she watched the storm in its full fury. It sounded more like rocks were falling on the roof instead of water, and the rain was like a thick gray sheet of plastic. She'd certainly seen rough weather before, but nothing like this. This storm was violent, but worse, it was dangerous.

At least Emma was safe in town with Jessica and Jared. Jessica had called a few minutes ago as the rain had started and said she would bring Emma home in the morning.

But where was Jake? He never would have stayed out in this kind of rain. It was much too risky. He might be stubborn and mule-headed, but he wasn't stupid.

Something was wrong.

She knew it. She could feel it, deep down inside. It was a feeling that couldn't be explained, but it was real just the same. And it scared the hell out of her.

She couldn't just stand here and wait. She had to do *something*. But what? She knew the general area he was working in. Ever since the fire in the shed, he'd made a point to let her know where he'd be if she needed him. He'd also made a point to leave her the truck, just in case there was an emergency and she needed a vehicle.

Lightning flashed, illuminating the dark sky; thunder rattled the roof. How would she ever find him in this storm?

Savannah drew a sharp breath. She *had* to find him. And standing here wondering how was a waste of precious time.

Decision made, she ran to the front door, grabbed the truck keys off the table with one hand and her coat off the rack with the other. Rain hammered at her as she sprinted to the truck and jumped inside. It had taken her less than twenty seconds and she was already drenched. Water dripped from her shaking hand as she turned the ignition key and shoved the truck into gear.

The wipers had little effect on keeping the windshield clear, but somehow the staccato *whish-whish* helped keep Savannah focused. She white-knuckled the steering wheel, splashing through the mud while she scanned the area for any sign of Jake or his horse. One mile passed. Then two.

Nothing. Absolutely nothing but mesquite and mud and a few scattered trees. The truck bumped and clattered over the rough terrain.

What if she missed him and he was back at the ranch already? Or holed up somewhere safe and sound, waiting for the worst of it to pass? He'd be furious with her for taking a chance like this. Maybe she should go back and just wait.

No. He was out here. The feeling was too strong for her to ignore. He'd just have to be angry if she was wrong. She had to follow her instincts, and her instincts told her he needed her help.

Another half mile passed with no sign of Jake. Savannah bit her lip, torn between going back and moving forward. If she got out too far, she might not make it back.

Jake, dammit, where are you?

There! Her heart caught in her throat as she spotted movement under a tree several yards away. Was it Jake? She drove closer.

No. She gripped the wheel tighter in frustration. Just a few cows.

She started to drive by, then slammed on the brakes and slid in the fresh mud.

Jake's horse.

She'd almost missed it behind the cows, but his horse was there. Without Jake. That meant he was here, close by. He never would have left his horse. She honked the horn several times, then tugged on her jacket as she jumped out of the truck.

The sound of rushing water drew her to the edge of a ravine. She'd ridden to this area several times and knew there was a dry riverbed here. But it certainly wasn't dry at the moment. Water swelled through the ravine and, at the rate it was going, would probably overflow the banks before long.

Dear God, what if Jake—

Like a camera flash, another burst of lightning streaked across the sky, reflecting off the rushing water and outlining the landscape in brilliant silver.

That was when she saw him. No more than a muddy shape a few feet from her, Savannah spotted a man's figure, half in the water, his arms wrapped around a huge tree root.

"Jake!" she screamed.

As she scrambled down the muddy bank, she felt a rush of relief that she'd found him, and at the same time, terror that he was hurt. Her feet sank ankle deep in the mud, and she felt as if she was in a horrible dream, moving in slow motion. *Please let him be all right, please...*

"Jake!" she screamed again, but there was no movement. When she reached his side, she put her hands on his shoulders and hollered at him. He lifted his head slowly, blinking hard as he stared at her with dazed eyes. His hair was plastered against his head, and she could see an angry gash on his left temple that oozed blood. Savannah's heart slammed in her chest.

"What the hell are you doing here?" he mumbled hoarsely.

She knew he intended his comment as a reprimand, but there was no bite to it. "I'm saving your butt," she yelled over the roar of the water. "Now pull it together, Stone, and help me."

He nodded slowly, but his first attempt to move only resulted in his slipping down a foot. The water lifted his body and pulled at it, nearly sucking him away. Savannah screamed his name, then braced herself on the tree root and grabbed hold of his jacket, reining him in. His hands grasped the root, but he hadn't the strength to pull himself free of the water and climb up. Savannah knew there was no way she could pull him out herself, either. He was far too heavy for her, and between the incline and the mud, she couldn't get a good enough grip on him.

She yelled at him again. "I'm going to get a rope. You hold on, Jake Stone, or so help me, I'll hang you with it!"

She ran to Jake's horse, her feet alternately slipping and sticking in sludgy ground. Saucy shied away as Savannah grabbed for the reins and tied the rope to the saddle horn, but followed easily when she was led back to the ravine. Savannah knew that the animal was well trained; she only prayed that the horse would obey someone other than Jake.

Jake was where she'd left him, facedown. The rope was already in her hands as she scrambled down to him and lifted his head, calling his name until he opened his eyes. He looked more like some kind of creature emerging from the muck than a handsome six-foot-four man. Savannah's heart caught in her throat as she wiped the wet earth from his face. She desperately wanted to pull him into her arms, but she had to get him out of here first.

Slipping the rope under his arms, she tied the best knot she could with wet shaky hands, then stood, motioning for Saucy to back up as she'd seen Jake do that day at the mud hole. The horse just stood and stared blankly. Desperate, Savannah swore at it, praying that the familiar expletives would make the animal respond. They didn't.

A loud crack had Savannah whirling back toward Jake. The tree root had split and Jake had slipped down in the water, his chin barely breaking the surface. One hand clung to the thread-thin root while the current played tug-of-war with his limp body.

"Jake!" She screamed again. He lifted his head and even through the pouring rain she saw the sudden determination that flashed in his eyes. He lifted his free hand from the water and gestured to the horse.

Amazingly the horse responded, whether from Jake's signal or the tightening of the rope, she wasn't sure, but in any event, the animal backed up, slowly reeling Jake in from the raging current. Savannah hurried to his side, dragging him upward until they both fell over the top of the bank.

Breathing hard, they lay there for a moment in each other's arms, the rain pounding down on them. Jake shook his head, and when he looked at Savannah, the glazed look in his eyes had cleared.

He lifted a hand to his brow and winced. "I lost my hat, dammit," he said weakly.

She laughed and cried at once. "Yeah, that was my first thought, too. Now let's get out of here."

They struggled to their feet and Savannah wrapped an arm around Jake's waist. Once she'd helped him into the truck, she ran back for Saucy and tied her to the bumper. Slowly, carefully, she drove back to the ranch.

Rain drummed on the roof of the cab, and the windshield wipers thunked back and forth. It felt as if the truck was hitting every dip and pothole as they inched their way back. Jake stared ahead, water dripping from his tightly clenched jaw.

"Your forehead is bleeding," she said quietly.

Jake touched his hand to his temple and swore when he pulled away bloodstained fingers. "I guess my head isn't as hard as some people think."

She ignored his comment and concentrated on her driving. It seemed like hours, but it was truly only a few minutes before Savannah stopped the truck in front of the barn. Once Saucy was taken care of, she and Jake walked slowly to the house, despite the fact it was still pouring rain. They were both so tired and wet they didn't care.

"We're too filthy to go in the front," Jake said, and led Savannah around to the back door. Inside the small laundry room and porch area, the boots came off first, then Jake's shirt and Savannah's jacket.

Savannah looked down at herself and groaned. She was covered with mud, nearly as much as Jake. "It's hard to believe people pay money to take baths in this muck," she said with disgust.

It suddenly dawned on Savannah that they were both going to have to strip. Right here. In front of each other. When Jake reached for the button on his jeans, she turned away, her face hot.

"This is no time for modesty, Savannah," he said wearily. "I have no intention of sitting around here all day until we dry. We've both got to get into a hot shower."

She glanced at him sharply. He grinned as he pulled his zipper down. "You can go first."

They left their clothes in a dirty heap on the laundry-room floor. Savannah, in her bra and panties, padded to the bathroom while Jake, in his briefs, followed close behind.

She stood outside the bathroom, hugging her arms to her. "You go first," she insisted.

He frowned at her. "You're shaking so hard your teeth are rattling. You go first."

She shook her head. "You're the one who almost died, Jake. You go."

He clenched his jaw and started to turn away, then abruptly turned back and grabbed her arm. She gasped as he pulled her into the bathroom. "This is ridiculous. We've both seen each other, Savannah, and I'm too damn tired to jump you right now, anyway."

"Jake—"

She gave a little shriek as he scooped her off her feet and set her in the shower. He stepped in with her, then turned on the water. It sprayed out hot and steamy and felt so good that, despite the circumstances, Savannah relaxed a little.

The bottom of the tub turned brown as the mud washed off them. Jake stuck his head under the shower head, then moved out of the way for Savannah to do the same. She felt silly showering with her underwear on, but as flimsy as it was, it still offered a tiny bit of comfort. Jake, however, was not so bashful. He tugged off his briefs and soaped his entire body. Her throat went dry at the magnificent sight of him, and she had to tear her gaze away before he caught her openly staring at him.

He was true to his word, though, and never once made a move toward her. Or even looked at her, she realized, with a strange mixture of relief and disappointment.

After they dried off, Jake wrapped a towel around his hips and Savannah around her torso. He started to leave the bathroom, but she took hold of his arm.

"Sit here," she said, flipping down the toilet lid. "I want to look at that cut over your eye."

He looked in the mirror. Blood seeped from the gash, which was starting to darken to a purplish blue. "It's just a scratch, for God's sake. I can—"

"Sit." She pointed at the makeshift medical seat.

With a heavy sigh, Jake gave in to Savannah's firm request. From the determined look on her face, he realized he had little choice. The pain from the cut was minimal, though. Nothing compared to the pain he'd just experienced taking a shower with the woman. Just knowing she was inches away from him, nearly naked, had his stomach in knots. He hadn't dared to look at her once or he would have lost it completely.

He watched her now as she bustled about the bathroom, grabbing hand towels from the linen closet, then antiseptic and bandages from the medicine cabinet. Her skin glowed from the hot water and her cheeks were flushed.

When she bent over him and cleaned his wound with a hot washcloth, he swore between clenched teeth.

"Does this scratch hurt?" she asked with sweet sarcasm.

He glared at her. Her fingers worked over him, and when she applied the antiseptic, he jerked away and swore again.

She frowned at him and took hold of his chin with her hand. "I can't do this if you don't sit still, Jake. Concentrate on something else."

That wasn't a difficult request, though he doubted she'd intended his thoughts to stray where they did. Her hand was soft and warm against his chin, and without thinking she'd worked her body between his legs. He stared at the soft white mound of flesh just above the knot on her towel and felt himself start to harden. He could pull that knot out with his teeth, then take the firm peak of her breast into his mouth...

When she leaned even nearer, he closed his hands into fists.

"It's almost stopped bleeding," she murmured, her brows drawn sharply together as she examined the cut.

Her hair was a mass of wet curls around her pale face and the scent of peaches filled his senses. Her knee brushed against his thigh and he sucked in a sharp breath. The storm raging outside was like a drizzle compared to the storm raging inside him. "You shouldn't have gone out there, Savannah," he said gruffly.

Her delicate brows lifted as she reached for a bandage.

"A thank-you might be more appropriate. You'd be doing the backstroke right now if it wasn't for me."

He needed to hold on to some of his anger or else he'd be pulling her into his arms. "A storm like this is dangerous, Savannah. What if something had happened to you? Did you ever think about Emma?"

She went perfectly still, then drew a slow breath. Her fingers were shaking as she pressed the bandage on. "I obviously wasn't thinking at all," she said tightly. "I assure you it won't happen again."

She started to turn away, but he grabbed her wrist. "Savannah, I'm—"

"I'd leave that on for a couple of days," she interrupted him. "It shouldn't get infected, but you'll probably have a scar."

"Savannah, don't. I didn't mean—"

"You'll probably have a doozy of a headache, too, so—"

"Savannah. Stop it." He pulled her to him, and when her knees started to buckle he hauled her onto his lap. She didn't resist, just laid her head against his shoulder and trembled. He felt like an idiot, being so harsh with her when she'd just saved his life.

"I'm sorry," he whispered against her neck. "The thought of anything happening to you scares the hell out of me."

"I didn't think of Emma," she said so quietly he could barely hear her. "I was thinking about you."

He brushed the wet hair away from her face. "Thank you."

She smiled weakly. "You're welcome."

He couldn't help but think how well she fitted against him. He tightened his hold on her and she snuggled against him.

"You almost died, Jake," she whispered so softly he could barely hear her.

"I didn't."

She pulled away and looked into his eyes. "But you could have. How can you live like this? Face this kind of danger every day?"

He laughed softly. "Funny, when the security guard at your town house had to open those gates for me, I asked myself the same question about you."

She smiled, then nodded slowly in understanding. Her eyes softened as she touched his cheek with her fingers. "Don't let it happen again. Emma needs both of her big brothers."

He wanted to ask her what *she* needed, but he already knew the answer. It was the one thing he couldn't give her.

He had three days before Savannah and Emma left. Time was a precious commodity, and after what had nearly happened to him this afternoon, he realized he didn't want to waste one minute of that time.

Savannah sighed at the feel of Jake's hand moving gently up her back. He'd nearly died this afternoon, and here he was, comforting her. She might have laughed at the thought, but the tiny circles he was making with his fingers overrode the myriad emotions coursing through her.

What had Digger said about standing between raindrops and keeping dry? It was impossible. Literally and figuratively. She loved Jake, and it was just as impossible for her to deny that.

She didn't want to think anymore of what was right or wrong. It simply was, and she accepted it. She leaned into him with a sudden desperate need to feel him closer. His lips brushed her forehead, and she felt as if she were turning to liquid. No one before Jake had ever made her feel this way before. No one ever would again.

His hot breath fanned her cheek and he whispered her name. He'd brought the storm in with him; she could smell it on him, feel it in the air that surrounded them. Her heart was pounding as furiously as the rain on the roof, and when she lifted her face to his, his mouth closed over hers in a kiss more powerful than ten storms.

She moaned into his mouth, meeting the thrust of his tongue with her own. His arms closed around her, pulling her tightly against him. He tasted her, and she him, again and again, with an urgency that left them both gasping.

He tugged her towel away.

Jake's hand moved up her spine and she arched her back, biting her bottom lip as his mouth closed over her breast, sucking at her through the thin lace of her damp bra. His teeth lightly raked her nipple, and she felt the heat of his breath on her skin. Sensation after sensation shimmered through her, and a knot of passion deep within tightened and loosened, tightened and loosened, alternately turning pleasure to pain and pain to pleasure.

He unsnapped the front clip of her bra and pushed the thin lace out of his way. His tongue traced the outer softness of her nipple, then the pebbled tip itself. Her fingers raked through his wet hair and over his shoulders. His muscles rippled and bunched under her fingers.

His mouth caught hers again and he stood, bringing her up with him and setting her on the edge of the counter.

"Touch me, Savannah." His breath was ragged. "I need to feel your hands on me."

His eyes, dark with passion, closed when she laid her hands on his chest. She could feel the thunder of his heartbeat. She pressed her mouth to his skin, and the masculine taste of him aroused her even more. He shuddered as she moved over him, exploring the hard planes and valleys of his muscles. She felt a power she'd never known before, a strength she'd never dreamed she'd possessed.

His hands cupped her bottom and he pulled her against him, pressing his arousal tightly against her. She started to pull the towel from his sleek lean hips and remove the terrycloth barrier between them, but he pushed her hand away and lifted her in his arms, holding her gaze with his as he carried her into the bedroom. He lowered her until her feet touched the floor and, with his eyes still locked with hers, slowly removed her panties, then tugged the towel from his hips.

Lightning flashed, bathing the room in silver. Thunder rumbled. She watched as he turned and reached into the nightstand. Was it the storm? Savannah wondered a moment later as he eased her gently back onto the bed and slid into her. Or was it the force of their lovemaking?

He whispered her name and liquid heat poured through her, setting her skin on fire. He moved slowly inside her, painfully slow, and she whimpered her distress. Didn't he know how badly she needed him? She moved her hands over him, tempting him to hurry, begging him to hurry, but he ignored her, taking his time. It was maddening. It was exquisite.

At last, his own desire became as uncontrolled as hers. His hands held her hips tightly against him and he thrust wildly, powerfully. She matched him, and he filled her, not just with his body, but with his very soul.

And when the coiling tension inside her exploded, she screamed his name, arching her body into his. He crushed her to him, groaning deeply, his rigid body shaking with the force of his release.

She held him tight, hanging on not only to Jake, but the moment.

The rain settled to a gentler, but steady downpour. Jake listened to the soothing sound of the quieting storm and realized he must have fallen asleep. Savannah was asleep, as well, nestled in the crook of his arm, her head on his shoulder and her warm body flush with his.

He'd never been so thankful for a storm in all his life.

He gathered her closer to him, refusing to think about what might have happened if she hadn't found him this afternoon. She had, and that was all that mattered. He'd face a dozen storms if this was where they led.

She stirred and slipped a long leg over his. The movement made his breath catch and he marveled at how soft and smooth she was, how right it felt to hold her like this, as if she'd been made to fit exactly him, only him.

"You awake?" he asked quietly.

"Hmm." She pressed her mouth to his chest and her fingers moved over him, soft as a whisper, hot as a branding iron. His pulse jumped, then raced as her lips moved downward and caressed the sensitive skin of his stomach.

"Savannah..."

His fingers closed over her shoulders and he sucked in a sharp breath. Her tongue glided over him, tasting, probing, setting his blood on fire. The outside world fell away and there was nothing but increasing sensation. His eyes shut and his breathing grew harsh and ragged.

Her teeth lightly raked his skin, then nipped. She moved over him and her hair fell across his stomach like a silken curtain. Pleasure, more concentrated and more intense than he'd ever known, radiated through him. It was impossible to think. All he could do was feel.

His hunger for her drove him wild. With a sharp exclamation, he pulled her upward and dragged her beneath him. She wrapped her legs around him as he moved deeply inside her, and he heard her call his name over and over.

Her moan shredded the last of his control. Thunder and lightning and flash floods were child's play compared to the explosion shattering his senses. Savannah clung to him as he cried out, and they were as one when the shock wave vibrated from his body to hers.

When the world righted again, the room was swathed in darkness. Jake heard the heavy beat of his heart over the sound of the rain and felt the gentle rise and fall of Savannah's breathing. She lay beside him, her head on his outstretched arm.

"Are you all right?" he asked her when he was capable of speech again.

Her quiet sigh made him smile. Her lips on his throat made him groan. He tugged her closer.

"I never knew I enjoyed the rain so much," she said breathlessly.

His smile deepened. "Sometimes it rains for days."

"Really?" Her hand caressed his thigh. "How long do you think this one will last?"

He chuckled and turned sideways, fitting her to him as he slid his hand along her hip. "Through the night, at least."

Not long enough, Savannah thought. Not nearly long enough. "What do you usually do when it rains like this?"

His thumb stroked the side of her breast. "Think about doing what I'm doing now."

The rough texture of his thumb against her soft flesh made her breath catch. "I'm being serious. What do you do when you have spare time? You don't even have a TV."

He laughed dryly. "I had one. My ex-wife threw our wedding picture through it the day she left. I just never got around to replacing it."

Her hand slid up his arm. "Myrna said that your wife was surprised when you served her with divorce papers."

He stiffened slightly at the mention of Myrna's name. "That woman's head is stuffed with feathers."

"Your father married her."

"Like I told you, lonely men make mistakes."

"Is that why you got married?" she asked carefully. "You were lonely?"

He moved away from her then, sitting up in bed. When he reached over and turned on the bedside lamp, a soft glow filled the room. She watched the muscles in his back ripple as he raked a hand through his tousled hair.

"When I was twenty-nine, Myrna gave a birthday party for my father. Of course, she invited *her* friends, not J.T.'s. Carolyn, my ex, had come to the party with her father, a wealthy stockbroker from Houston. She was beautiful and funny and I wanted to be in love. I wanted to settle down, have kids. I thought that's what she wanted, too."

He stared at the round brass clock on the nightstand and watched the second hand sweep silently around the dial. "I never really understood why she married me. I was a novelty to her, I think. A far cry from the lawyers and stockbrokers she'd been dating."

Savannah had dated men like that. Most of them were boring and preoccupied with the kind of car they drove or the fit of their custom-made suits. It was hard for her to imagine any woman preferring that type of man to Jake.

"It was okay the first year," he went on. "She kept telling me she wanted to have kids right away. We talked about the future. But the isolation out here and the difference in our life-styles got to her. She started to complain that I never spent any time with her, that I couldn't drop my work and fly off to Florida or New York for a party. She started to travel by herself." He sighed heavily. "We argued. The trips got longer and more frequent. I finally gave her an ultimatum. No more trips, and I wanted children."

"Two months later I came in early one day. There was a note she'd gone into Midland and would be back late. At ten o'clock I was getting ready to go look for her on the highway when the phone rang. It was Sam. Carolyn was at his house. She was sick and hadn't been able to make the drive back to the ranch."

"Sick?"

Jake's face lost all expression as he lifted his gaze to Savannah. "She'd gone into Midland to have an abortion."

An abortion. Oh, God. Savannah felt her stomach rise and shift. The hollow look in Jake's eyes brought a tightness to her throat. "I'm sorry," she whispered.

"I'd known she was angry, that she was unhappy, but I never dreamed she'd try to get back at me that way."

Savannah moved toward him and covered his hand with her own. His knuckles were white where he clutched the sheet. "She was a fool," she said softly.

"I might have killed her if Sam hadn't stopped me. I took my anger out on him, instead. I even accused him of sleeping with her. Lord knew, she'd flirted with him enough to make even the most apathetic husband jealous."

So that was the edge between Jake and Sam, Savannah realized. Only it was obvious that Sam had forgiven Jake. It was Jake who couldn't forgive himself.

"Family was always something I regarded as sacred," Jake said, his lips held tight. "No matter what, you stuck together, worked your problems out. In the blink of an eye, Carolyn destroyed that. I realized that other than my father, the only true family I'd ever have would be Jared and Jonathan and Jessica. When Jonathan died six months later, I realized how tenuous life itself is. I wasn't going to waste it on any more mistakes."

Is that what she was to Jake? Savannah wondered. A mistake? Pain sliced through her. He wanted a woman in his bed, but would never give her his name or his heart. He would never risk loving her as she loved him.

She wouldn't settle for less than that. Not from Jake.

Some folks don't even find that kind of love once.

A hollow ache settled in her stomach as she remembered Digger's words when he'd told her about Angela and J.T. Savannah knew that she had found that kind of love, that kind of passion. And if she and Jake only had these next few days together, then she would accept that. She didn't want them to part angrily. For Emma's sake, she and Jake would have to at least be friends.

Friends? Her body was still humming from their love-making. She doubted she would ever associate the word "friend" with Jake.

She held back the sigh at the base of her throat and moved closer to Jake, laying her cheek on his shoulder. He stiffened, and she knew that inwardly he was busy rebuilding a wall that had just fallen between them. If she hurried, she might slip beyond the crumbling barrier, and even if it was only for this one night, he might let her in. She turned him toward her and pressed her mouth to his as she guided him back onto the bed, brushing his lips with hers in a kiss intended to seduce, as well as heal. He grabbed her head between his hands and put her away, staring down at her with a distant cool look that tore at her heart.

She held his gaze, refusing to back down. His blue eyes darkened with desire, and with a low growl, he dragged her against him, slanting his mouth against hers, searing her with his lips again and again.

She met the thrust of his tongue with a passion of her own, knowing that from this day on, whenever it rained, she would remember this moment and how much she loved the man in her arms.

Eleven

Jake stood in the doorway, unnoticed, watching Savannah pack the last of her things in her suitcase. Her flight wasn't scheduled to leave for another four hours, but with the two-hour drive into Midland, she and Emma would need to leave soon.

He was still smarting from her polite refusal of his offer to drive her and Emma to the airport. She'd asked Jessica and Jared, instead. She'd told him she didn't want to take him away from his work, but they both knew the real reason: it was too damn hard to say goodbye.

A knot formed in his stomach as he watched her fold the pink blouse she'd been wearing the day of the Roundup. He could still remember the way her face had lit up when Emma had won that blue ribbon and the spontaneous hug she'd given him. When she placed the blouse in the suitcase and smoothed her slender hands over the fabric, Jake felt the knot tighten.

"Savannah."

Startled, she turned. Something flickered in her green eyes, but it was too brief to recognize. The look she gave him now was reserved.

"I'm just finishing up," she said, and reached for a small floral cosmetics bag on the bed. "Emma's gone out to the barn to see Betsy before we leave. You might want to say goodbye to her out there where you can be alone."

He didn't want to say goodbye at all, dammit. Jake moved into the room and stared down at Savannah's suitcase. What he wanted to do was dump everything out and throw the damn bag through the window.

He shoved his hands into his pockets. "We haven't talked about visits." When she looked at him, he added, "With Emma."

She turned away and placed the cosmetics bag in her suitcase. "Jessica has offered to keep Emma with her in town on any future trips."

"I don't understand." Jake watched her close the suitcase, and when she snapped the lock, he had that same sinking feeling he'd had when the security gates at Savannah's town house had clanked shut behind him.

"We can arrange visits based on Emma's school schedule and holidays." She straightened and met his gaze straight on. "I won't be coming with her, Jake."

The knife already sticking in his gut twisted. He should have known. He'd just hoped that after they'd made love that last time that . . . that she might want to . . .

Oh, hell. He was a fool to think she might change her mind. She'd told him exactly what she intended to do. Find a nice dependable husband and settle into a nice dependable life.

So let her. She'd find out soon enough there was no such thing as stable or dependable. The entire concept was one big fraud.

Anger, as dark as it was unreasonable, shot through him, and with tremendous effort he controlled it. "I'll carry your bags out for you."

She shook her head. "I can manage. I'll just say good-bye now, Jake."

He watched in stunned disbelief as she stuck her hand out. The image of her slender body under his when they'd made love, her legs wrapped around him, came to his mind.

And she wanted to shake hands?

To hell with that.

He grabbed her and hauled her against him. He'd give her a goodbye she'd never forget, he thought, intending his kiss to be more punishment than pleasure. He caught her startled gasp with his mouth, and when her palms came up against his chest, he fully expected her to push away from him. Instead, her hands slid upward and she wound her arms around his neck, lifting up on her toes as she leaned into him.

He deepened the kiss, slanting his mouth hard against hers, knowing that the only punishment in this was to himself, and he was the one who would never forget this goodbye. He poured every feeling in him into the kiss, telling her with his mouth how he felt. Passion and need and desire. All of that burned within him. He felt her tremble in his arms, but when he moved to pull her closer, she stumbled away, her eyes wide and bright with what he thought were tears.

"Goodbye, Jake," she whispered hoarsely, and turned away.

He started to take a step toward her, then clenched his jaw and stopped. The thought that he'd almost begged her to stay shocked him. The thought that he still might infuriated him. He walked out of the room, and when he slammed the front door on his way to the barn, the house shook from the force of it.

Her heart pounding, Savannah sank onto the edge of the bed and closed her eyes, waiting for her world to stop spinning. When she could breathe again, she raised a shaking hand to her mouth and pressed her fingers to her lips. They still burned from Jake's kiss.

Damn you, Jake Stone.

He hadn't even let her leave with her dignity. Her entire body ached for him, and she knew that if he'd asked her to stay she would have. And if she had, she would have ended up hating herself for it, and then maybe even Jake, too.

She drew a slow deep breath and stood. It had to be like this. She'd never stand in the way of his relationship with Emma; she knew he loved the child as much as she did. As a newly accepted member of the Stone family, Emma would never be at a loss for love or care, and that thought gave Savannah comfort. Despite the pain that permeated every inch of her body, Savannah knew that, for Emma's sake, this trip had been worth every minute.

She continued with her packing, listening to the bedside clock loudly tick away the seconds. They'd be back in Atlanta in a few hours, and Stone Creek would just be a place, instead of a home.

The sound of Jake's truck starting and screeching away brought a sharp stab to Savannah's stomach. She'd see him again sometime, because of Emma. But they'd be no more than polite strangers by then. Each of them would have moved on with his and her own life.

And that's what she intended to do, she thought firmly. Move on with her life. It was time to look forward, for her future, as well as Emma's.

She was closing her second suitcase when the roar of an engine caught Savannah's attention. Jake? It couldn't be. He'd already left. *Unless he'd come back* . . . Her pulse racing, Savannah hurried to the window, praying that it was Jake, that he had come back.

A white luxury sedan pulled out from behind the barn and she felt her heart sink. It wasn't Jake. It was Myrna.

Savannah closed her eyes and groaned out loud. Of all the people she didn't want to see right now, Myrna was number one on the list.

But the car was leaving, not coming, Savannah noted, narrowing her eyes as she watched the vehicle disappear. *Thank goodness.* She let out a sigh of relief and decided not to question her good fortune. Neither she nor Emma needed to deal with Jake's stepmother today.

Savannah suddenly realized that her niece hadn't returned from the barn yet. She glanced at the bedside clock. Jessica and Jared would be here any minute, and Emma still needed to change into her traveling clothes.

Frowning, Savannah moved away from the window and headed for the front door, knowing she was going to have to drag her niece away from that calf. Emma had gone to bed in tears the night before because she hadn't wanted to leave, and Savannah knew they were probably in for a scene again now.

Not that Savannah blamed the child. Lord knew, she felt like kicking and screaming herself.

Her hand was on the front doorknob when she heard Emma's scream. She flew out the door and off the front porch, her heart hammering at the terror she heard in her niece's voice.

Oh, my God! No!

Smoke billowed from the open barn doors.

"Emma!" Savannah shouted. "Get out of the barn!"

There was no response, only the sound of Emma's sobbing and the furious screams of the frightened horses. Savannah stumbled and nearly fell, but she recovered quickly. Her feet barely touched the ground as she raced into the barn.

The thick acrid smoke burned her eyes, making it difficult to see. "Emma! Where are you?"

"I'm here! With Betsy," she shrieked from the end stall, coughing as she spoke.

Using her hands more than her eyes, Savannah made her way toward Emma. "I'm coming, sweetie," she said, struggling to keep the panic from her voice. "Everything will be fine."

It has to be. She couldn't consider anything else.

Savannah heard the flames crackle behind her and thanked God that the fire was at the other end of the barn.

Tears streaked down her cheeks, blurring her vision even more.

She called Emma's name again, but there was no answer. The smoke was so thick now Savannah wasn't sure where she was anymore, but the sound of a bell ringing—Betsy's bell!—helped guide her. As she passed by the stalls with the horses, she unlatched the gates and swung them open. There were only three occupied, and the animals reared up when she waved her arms and hollered at them. Grunting in fear, they bolted past her. As it cleared the stall, the last horse knocked Savannah on the shoulder, throwing her to the ground. Pain shot through her back and stole her breath. Stars danced in front of her eyes.

Dazed, she lay there, gasping, then choking as she pulled the thick air into her burning lungs. She shook her head to clear it.

Jake, where are you? She prayed he'd see the smoke and return. As angry as he'd been, he might have driven halfway across Texas by now, without looking back once.

She couldn't think about him now. Emma's—and her own life—depended on her staying focused and calm.

She struggled to her feet, forcing her trembling legs to move as she followed the sound of the calf's bell. She found Emma huddled in the corner of the stall, her arms around Betsy's neck.

"Emma!" Savannah fell to her knees and gathered her shaking niece close.

"I'm scared," Emma sobbed.

I am, too. Savannah stood, dragging Emma with her. "Hurry, sweetie. We've got to get out of here."

Betsy bawled loudly when Emma left her. "What about Betsy?" Emma cried and pulled back.

Savannah caught her niece by the shoulders. "Emma, we've got to go!"

"We can't leave her here. Please, Aunt Savannah!"

There was no possible way Savannah could carry the animal out. She hadn't the strength or the time. But if she didn't bring the calf, Emma's protest would cost them time, too. The smoke had thickened, and the sound of the crackling fire seemed to surround them. "Does she have a lead rope?"

Emma nodded, then groped for the rope in the hay. "I put it on her when I smelled the smoke, but she wouldn't come."

"All right, hang on tight to me. I'll pull Betsy." The calf resisted the first tug of the line, but Savannah yanked harder and the animal yielded.

With the back of the barn in flames, the rear doors were impossible to reach. Their only escape was the front entrance. Savannah and Emma were both coughing as they felt their way toward the wide double doors.

The sound of wood cracking stopped them. Savannah watched in horror as a large beam crashed down over the barn doors and sent sparks flying. Emma screamed as Savannah protected the girl's body with her own.

Their only escape was suddenly and irrevocably cut off.

"Don't let go of me, Emma, no matter what," Savannah yelled over the fire. A wave of heat rolled over them, and she pulled her niece and Betsy back in the same direction they'd come.

She needed an ax, or some kind of tool. If she could break her way through the side of the barn, even a hole small enough for Emma, then at least her niece could—

She stopped, listening. Over the howl of the fire she heard a sound.

A horn honking!

Jake! It had to be! She recognized the truck's horn as it came again, insistent. Outside, from the front. It was louder, then louder still, bearing down on them.

"Emma!" She pulled the child as far to the side as possible.

The double doors of the barn seemed to explode. Wood flew. Savannah pressed Emma against the wall, shielding her body.

Gasping for air, Savannah turned back.

Jake had driven the truck right into the barn!

Savannah blinked hard to clear her burning eyes. She watched as Jake jumped from the cab, kicking debris out of the way. "Savannah! Emma!"

"Over here!"

His large hands reached through the thick dark smoke and grabbed Emma, then tossed her into the cab of the truck. Savannah picked her way through the splintered wood, tugging on Betsy's rope. The animal protested, but Jake lifted the calf and in one fluid movement had her in the truck bed. Savannah cried out as Jake snatched her up, as well, and heaved her into the cab.

"Hang on!" Jake yelled. He threw the pickup into reverse and floored it. The truck lurched backward with the crunch of metal and cracking wood. Savannah pulled Emma tightly against her and muffled the child's scream against her chest.

Jake stopped the truck well out of harm's way. As he pulled Emma and Savannah out of the cab, all Savannah could hear was the sound of the roaring fire. She glanced at the barn, and a wall of flames engulfed the building.

"The horses," she whispered, but it was more like a rasp. Her lungs ached.

He set them both gently down on the ground and knelt beside them. "They got out."

Savannah closed her eyes in relief, opening them again when Emma began to cough. She held her niece against her, rocking her until the spasm passed.

The barn roof collapsed and the ground shook.

"Oh, Jake," she said weakly, tears choking the back of her raw throat. "Your barn."

Ashes swirled through the air and slowly drifted to the ground.

He glanced over his shoulder at what was left of the structure. A muscle jumped in his clenched jaw. "Never mind the barn. The only thing that matters is that you and Emma are all right."

Betsy bawled from the back of the truck. Jake lifted the calf out of the bed and placed her beside Emma, who started to cry as she threw her arms around the animal.

"I didn't do it, Jake," Emma sobbed. "I didn't start the fire. I was just saying goodbye to Betsy."

"I never thought you did, sweetheart," Jake said softly and brushed Emma's hair from her soot-and-tear-covered face. "Sometimes things like this just happen."

"Savannah! Emma! Oh, my God, are you all right?"

Savannah turned. Jessica left her car door open as she jumped from the station wagon and ran toward them, her eyes wide. Jared was right behind her, his face tight with worry.

"We're fine," Savannah said, but she coughed at the effort the words cost her. Light-headed, she leaned against the side of the truck. Spots swam in front of her eyes. "I'd appreciate it if you'd take care of Emma, though. I'm . . . feeling a little . . ."

She never finished the sentence before the darkness closed around her.

"Hell of a day," Jared said to Jake two hours later as he handed him a shot of whiskey. "I'd say you've earned yourself a drink."

"Day's not over yet." Jake paused just long enough in his pacing to down the liquid, then hand the glass back to his brother. "Save the bottle."

Jake felt his brother's silent gaze follow him as he continued to pace the length of the living room. He hadn't changed his soot-streaked clothes yet, and he could smell the stench of smoke on himself.

"What the hell is that doctor doing in there?" Jake glanced toward the bedrooms. "Playing Monopoly?"

Jared settled back on the couch and sipped at his own drink. "It hasn't been long, Jake."

Jake ran a shaky hand through his hair. He looked at his fingers, covered with ashes, then closed his eyes and swore. He felt Jared's hand on his shoulder.

"They're all right," Jared said quietly.

Jake opened his eyes and stared at his brother. "If I hadn't seen the smoke when I did, they'd have..."

"Life is full of *if*s." Jared's hand tightened on Jake's shoulder. "It'll only tear you up inside to think about them."

Jake sighed and nodded, realizing that no one knew that better than Jared. Savannah and Emma were alive.

That was all that mattered.

Jessica came out of the bedroom then, followed by Dr. Stanley Sanders, a portly man with gray sideburns.

Jake felt his heart hammering against his ribs as he moved toward the doctor. "Well?"

"Your ladies are fit as fiddles," Dr. Sanders said. "Lungs and eyes are clear, no contusions, burns or lacerations. I'd say they were mighty lucky."

Lucky? They almost died in a fire, for God's sake, Jake thought irritably. Still, he slowly released the breath he'd been holding. "Can I see them?"

"You can see Miss Roberts now, but Emma is sleeping." The doctor pushed his wire-frame glasses higher on his nose and took in Jake's ragged appearance. "How 'bout we have a look at you first, son?"

"Not necessary." He started to brush past the doctor, then stopped at the sound of a woman's voice calling him from outside.

Oh, God, no. Not Myrna.

His stepmother ran into the house, an expression of complete horror on her face. "Jake, what happened?"

"Maybe you can tell us, Mrs. Stone."

Jake whirled at the Southern voice that spoke from the hallway. Savannah. She was dressed in her robe, her jaw tightly set as she stared at Myrna.

"How could I tell you?" She looked confused. "I just drove in from town."

Savannah moved into the room, her hard gaze never leaving Myrna. "I saw your car driving away from here not more than two hours ago, just before the fire started."

Everyone in the room stared at Myrna. Her face paled against her red hair. "But I've been at the hairdresser's all morning. I just heard there was trouble out here when William picked me up."

William.

An alarm bell went off in Jake's head. Jared must have had the same thought, because they were both suddenly moving toward the front door.

The driver stood by the side of the car, arms folded, chewing at a toothpick as he kicked at the ground with the toe of his boot. He glanced up, and his eyes widened at the sight of the Stone brothers bearing down on him. Fear registered clearly on his face, and he glanced around as if he might run, but realized it would be futile.

"Hey, Jake, Jared," he said nervously. "Too bad about the barn."

Jake stood no more than a foot away from the man. He could smell the liquor on his breath. "Where were you two hours ago, Billy?"

The toothpick shifted from one corner of Billy's mouth to the other. "I, ah, was in town. Took Mrs. Stone there for her weekly hair appointment like I always do."

"So you don't know who might have set my barn on fire, then."

Billy's mouth tightened. "I told ya, I was in town. Everybody seen me. I was there when Mrs. Stone come out of the beauty shop."

"It takes an hour and a half to drive to town and back." Jake moved in closer still to the man, close enough to see the sweat bead on his forehead. "Myrna's appointments take at least that long. Where were you between the time you dropped her off and picked her up?"

"I had things to do." He shifted from one foot to the other.

"Like set fire to my barn?"

"Hey, I don't like what—"

Jake grabbed the front of the man's shirt and nearly lifted him off the ground. "I don't like my barn being burned down, either, Billy. You were seen here. Driving away just before the fire started."

The man's weak protest only increased Jake's anger. Rage built inside him, and he tightened his grip on Billy and shook him furiously. "My sister was in that barn," he said in what sounded like a low growl. "She might have died."

Billy's glazed eyes widened. The toothpick fell out of his mouth. "But Mrs. Stone said you was at the airport, that you were all gone. I checked—" The words had rushed out of his mouth like a dam breaking open before he stopped short and blinked, suddenly realizing all he'd said.

"What else did Mrs. Stone tell you?" Jake shook the man again. "To set fire to my barn? Like you did the shed?"

"I ain't saying nothing!" Billy yelled. "I want a lawyer."

"You'll get a lawyer." Jake's eyes narrowed. He shoved Billy against the car. "But first you're going to need this doctor I've got here."

He swung his arm back, and Billy doubled over as Jake's fist connected with his stomach. Jake was reaching for Billy again when Jessica moved beside him and placed a hand on his shoulder.

"Jake," she said anxiously, "I've called the sheriff. He'll be here soon."

His fist still raised, Jake turned and saw Savannah standing a few feet away, her face ashen as she watched. She'd seen enough for one day, he realized, and let his arm drop. He swore heatedly and shoved Billy to the ground.

"Get a rope, Jared," Jake said between clenched teeth. When Billy gasped, Jake smiled malevolently. "Don't worry, Billy. We'll save the hanging for later, when the whole town can watch."

"Jake." Myrna's voice was shaky as she stepped close. "I hope you don't think I had anything to do with this."

Anger jumped in Jake's temple as he stared at his step-mother. "What better way to get my land, Myrna, than to slowly drive me bankrupt? Losing my barn ought to put the last nail in my coffin."

"But I didn't . . . I would never hurt you that way. Or the child. My God." She swung around and faced Savannah. "You have to believe me. I was angry at Angela. I even hated her for taking J.T. away from me. But I never would have hurt the child. Not then, or now. I swear it."

"You knew?" Savannah's brow tightened and she took a step toward Myrna. "About J.T. and Angela?"

"He was going to divorce me," the woman whispered raggedly, and hugged her arms tightly to her. "He'd moved into the east wing and contacted a lawyer. I couldn't let him leave me. I couldn't."

It would have been easy to feel sorry for the woman, Savannah thought numbly. In her own way, Myrna had loved J.T., but not enough to let his happiness come before her own selfishness. "And the baby—you knew Angela was pregnant with J.T.'s child?"

Myrna pressed a shaky hand to her mouth and nodded again. "I had a friend who worked in the doctor's office."

The Stone children all stared at Myrna in disbelief. All those years she'd known and never told anyone, Savannah realized.

"If J.T. was divorcing you, why did Angela leave?" Jake asked.

Myrna straightened her shoulders and faced them all. "J.T. was *my* husband. She had no right to him. I did what I had to do to keep what belonged to me."

"And what was it you had to do?" Savannah asked carefully.

Myrna lifted her chin defiantly as she swung toward Savannah. "I told her *I* was pregnant. That J.T. and I were going to have the child we'd always talked about."

Jake swore. Savannah drew a sharp breath.

"She was pregnant, for God's sake!" Jake's eyes flashed in anger.

Myrna's lips trembled. "She was younger than me. Prettier. She could find someone else, even with a child. *I* needed J.T. Can't you understand?"

In desperation, Myrna looked at every face watching her. They all turned away, including Dr. Sanders.

"Jessica," Myrna choked out, "you understand, don't you? I loved your father. How could I let him leave me?"

Jessica shook her head and took the older woman by the arm. "I'll drive you home after the sheriff gets here," Jessica said quietly. "Let's go sit in the house now."

Myrna nodded slowly. "I know I've done some bad things, but I had nothing to do with the things that happened to Jake. Please believe me—I didn't."

"I believe you." Jessica looked at Jake, who frowned.

Savannah watched them walk away, trying to sort out the emotions ricocheting through her at the moment. *A lie.* Angela had sacrificed her love and denied her child a father because of a vicious lie.

She should feel better now that she knew the truth, Savannah told herself. But the only thing she felt was an emptiness, a sadness so profound it brought tears to her eyes. With a weary sigh, she turned on shaky legs and slowly walked back to the house.

An hour later, Jake knocked softly on Savannah's door. At her quiet response, he entered and found her standing at the window, arms folded, looking out toward the burned rubble that had been his barn. When he moved close to her and smelled the smoke still clinging to her hair, the image of the barn in flames came clearly to his mind, as did the feeling of terror when he realized that she and Emma were inside. A fresh wave of what-might-have-been shuddered through him.

And the realization hit him, stronger than any lightning bolt and more intense than any fire.

He loved her.

Loved her. The words rang through his head, and he had the craziest desire to shout them at her. He wanted to take her in his arms, pull her tightly to him and beg her to stay.

Beg her to marry him.

He started to reach for her, then drew his hand back.

What was the matter with him? He had nothing to offer Savannah now. The loss of his barn would cost him the ranch. He had no doubt about that. He was already too far behind financially. How could he ask her to marry him when he didn't even know where he'd be sleeping in a month?

What a cruel joke. He finally realized that he not only loved Savannah, but that she would never do anything his ex-wife had done. He knew he could trust her with his love and his life, and he couldn't offer her either one.

"What's going to happen now?" she asked, turning to face him.

She looked tired, he noted. He wanted to lay her down on the bed and gather her close to him. He wanted to listen to her heart beat as she slept and know she was all right. He couldn't do any of that.

"Billy's been arrested for setting the barn on fire," he said tightly. "It shouldn't take long to prove he also torched the shed, not to mention all the other problems the ranch has been having."

"But why?" Savannah asked.

"I wouldn't give him a recommendation to work on another ranch after I fired him for drinking. He had to resort to working for Myrna as a chauffeur. I suppose that's enough to drive anyone to desperation, but I never would have expected him to be so angry he'd go to the extremes he did to pay me back."

Savannah drew a weary breath. "And Myrna?"

Jake frowned. "The sheriff doesn't think she's involved. Unless Billy tells us different, she won't be charged with anything."

"What do you think?"

He sighed heavily. "Jessica and Jared don't think so, but by admitting she lied to your sister like she did proves she's capable of deceit."

"She loved J.T.," Savannah said softly. "She was wrong in what she did and I don't condone it, but I almost think I understand."

Jake shook his head. "J.T. had the right to know and to make his own decision. Myrna took that away from him."

The silence stretched tautly between them. From outside, Jake heard Jared shouting directions to some neighbors who had come by and offered help cleaning up.

"What about you, Jake?" Savannah asked quietly. "What are you going to do now?"

"I'll work something out with the bank," he said blithely. "I should have a new barn up by fall."

She looked at him, and he knew that she knew he was lying. Her eyes searched his and he saw the need there. The need for him to hold her and for her to hold him. He kept his distance.

"Emma and I could stay and help," she offered. He heard the hope in her voice, felt a spark of it himself.

Maybe, just maybe, with Savannah's help, I could do it. Work longer hours, get some work in town. If they were married...

He nearly laughed at the idea. What the hell was the matter with him? How long would she want to hang in there with a flat-broke rancher? He'd be gone all day, every day, and there weren't enough hours in any of those days to save this ranch. What kind of life was that to offer someone?

It was a stupid fantasy. He was only human, and he was tired. Damn tired. He'd lose this ranch whether Savannah was here or not. He wouldn't drag her—and Emma—down with him.

"Thanks, but I'll manage."

He saw the sharp hurt in her eyes. "I'm sure you will."

"Savannah—"

She turned her back on him and stared out the window again. "I think it's a good idea to let Emma rest today. There's another flight out tomorrow morning. I've already booked us on it." Her words were clipped and terse.

They'd been through this once today. He wouldn't have thought it could possibly hurt more than it already had. But it did. It hurt a hell of a lot more.

He turned and for the second time that day, walked out of Savannah Roberts's life.

Twelve

___

Jake stared at the letter in his hand, read it for the third time, then crumpled the stiff white paper between his fingers. He threw it across the room.

Dammit, dammit, *dammit!*

Fists clenched, jaw tight, he stood at the kitchen table, dragging in a deep breath to control the rage pouring through him.

Foreclosure.

The word was like a steel band closing around his chest, shutting off the air. There were other words, too. Like *We regret to inform you... policy of the bank... vacate in ten days.* Or the last line of the letter and the final insult—*If there's any way we may help...*

They could all take a flying leap, that might help, he thought angrily.

He moved stiffly to the sink, turned on the faucet full force and doused his face with cold water. He was hot and dirty and tired and in no mood to do battle with the bank.

Battle? he thought bitterly. Who was he kidding? He'd lost the battle more than a month ago when the barn had burned down.

When Savannah had left.

He would come in at night after working all day almost expecting to see her in the kitchen, humming along with the radio as she fixed dinner, or Emma's excited conversation as she related her day with Betsy or some other animal she'd managed to befriend.

Then he'd hear the silence and remember that they'd left, gone back to Atlanta, and a loneliness so intense would come over him it nearly strangled him.

God, how he missed them.

He wondered what they were doing right now. It was Friday, almost dinnertime. Was Savannah in her kitchen, humming? Was Emma telling her about her day?

Or was Savannah getting ready for a date, maybe slipping on some sleek sexy dress and high heels like the ones he'd seen her wearing the first time he'd met her? Unwillingly the image came of Savannah sitting in a fancy restaurant with some high-powered executive, laughing, smiling . . . then later, after dinner . . .

You're a damn fool, Jake Stone. You've already shot yourself in both feet. Why not go for the knees now?

Swearing, he splashed his face again, then shut the water off, nearly ripping the towel holder out of the wall as he dried his hands.

The wrinkled ball of paper glared at him from the counter where he'd thrown it.

Foreclosure.

Closing his eyes, he leaned back against the counter and sighed. He'd known it was coming, of course. It had been like waiting to hear about the friend who's been terminally ill. You wait and you hope. You deny. But the phone call comes and reality hits.

It's over.

He'd spent the last month applying for every loan conceivable in every bank imaginable. Money was tighter than a bobcat's tail, and the few banks that had talked to him had taken one look at his financial statement and shown him the door. The back door.

Ten days. He had ten days to get out. Ten days to gather up four generations of belongings and get the hell out before the vultures descended. Myrna would probably be the first bird of prey, he thought sourly.

At least the woman had been bright enough to stay out of his way for the past month. But good things never last, he told himself.

At least they never had for him.

He thought about Savannah again. Her green eyes fierce with determination when she'd defended Emma to Myrna, those same eyes wide with shock when she'd landed in the mud hole. And those same eyes again, heavy with passion when he'd made love to her.

And all he had left of her was the peach shampoo she'd forgotten in the shower. He'd left it there, whether to torture or comfort himself he wasn't sure. But the scent would drift up to him as he showered and he'd draw the fragrance into his lungs as if it were an invisible lifeline. If he closed his eyes, he could imagine she was still there, working beside him during the day, in his bed at night.

He turned to stare out the window, across the sweep of land that was his father's legacy to him. The land that once upon a time Jake had hoped would be his legacy to his children.

It was up to Jared and Jessica now to hold what was left of Stone Creek together. Jake had no doubt they'd succeed. He was proud of his brother and sister. They'd stood by each other, shared the pain of tragedy and the joy of happiness. They'd always been there for each other. They always would be.

So why did he feel so damn alone?

Let me stay and help you. He could still hear Savannah's quiet offer after the barn had burned down. He'd seen the hope in her eyes that he'd say yes to her. She'd truly wanted to stay, to help him rebuild.

God, how he'd wanted to say yes. For one foolish moment he'd actually thought that with her by his side he could do anything. Slay any dragon, overcome any obstacle.

Even hold on to this ranch.

Did she have any idea what she was asking? She'd be giving up her comfortable life in Atlanta to battle the weather and drought and a hundred other difficulties that were the way of life for ranchers. She'd been eager to help in the month she'd been here, and Lord knew she'd certainly survived the worst of storms. But how long would it be before that look of hope turned to disappointment, then disillusionment? The thought scared the hell out of him. How could he take that chance?

How could he not?

Jake stared at the letter from the bank, then thought about the bottle of whiskey he kept in his desk drawer. He'd planned on mending the fence between his and Sam's place this afternoon, but what the hell? There was no possible way in ten days he could come up with the kind of money he needed to keep the bank from moving in, so what was the point? The fence could stay down for all he cared.

He started for his office, then stopped suddenly.

The fence could stay down.

Maybe there was a way.

A strange calm settled over him. For the first time in a very long time, it became overwhelmingly clear to him what he had to do.

The office smelled of leather and dust and horsehair. The oak desktop was scarred from years of being used as a boot rest, and the walls were covered with family pictures. The finish had worn off the arms of the chairs, but the cushions were comfortable and designed to easily fit the long legs and arms of a tall man.

Jake sat in one of those chairs and looked at the man across from him.

"It's been a long time, Jake," Sam McCants said.

Jake nodded. "Too long, Sam."

Sam pulled a bottle of whiskey from the shelf behind him, then two shot glasses. "Business or social?"

"Both."

Sam filled the glasses and handed one to Jake. Without a word, both men downed the whiskey. The liquid burned Jake's tight throat.

"Let's start with social." Sam refilled the glasses.

Jake took the glass and stared at it. A big slice of pride took a while to chew, let alone swallow. "I owe you an apology."

Sam said nothing.

Jake's fingers tightened around the glass. "I know you never slept with Carolyn."

Sam's brows raised a fraction. "Took you almost four years to figure that out?"

Jake shook his head. "I knew it then. I just needed someone other than myself to be angry at."

"You mean someone you could hit?"

Jake closed his eyes. "I'm sorry about that, too."

Sam grinned and rubbed his chin. "You pack a hell of a right hook."

"You didn't deserve that."

"Yeah, well, you didn't deserve what you got, either."

Sam held his glass out and Jake touched it with his. The whiskey went down smoothly this time.

"So," Sam said, leaning back in his chair, "now that we have that out of the way, let's get on to the business."

"'We hold these truths to be self-evident,'" Savannah said, reciting the Declaration of Independence to the classroom, "'that all men are created equal...'"

She paused here, as an image of Jake popped into her mind. *Equal, yes,* she thought, *but certainly not the same.* She'd never met a more virile man than Jake.

Realizing that the children were staring at her, she blinked back to the present and continued, "'that they are endowed—'"

Good grief, yes, he most certainly—'"

Stop that! She frowned and shook the thought from her mind.

"'...by their creator,'" she moved on, "'with certain inalienable rights, that among these are life, liberty and the pursuit of happiness.'"

The pursuit of happiness. Savannah turned toward the blackboard and began writing the lesson so that sixteen nine-year-olds, including her own niece, wouldn't see a grown woman cry. When it came to her own life, the pursuit of happiness had wound up in a dead end.

The past month had gone by with painful slowness. Emma had been miserable since they'd come back from Texas. She'd picked at her food, neglected her friends and had been as sluggish as molasses on a cold day.

Which pretty much described herself, Savannah thought with a sigh.

The chalk squeaked across the board as she wrote, and the girls were restless in their seats waiting for her to finish. Joanie and Corrine were whispering and Sarah was giggling.

Savannah ignored the sounds, needing a moment to compose herself after letting Jake enter her thoughts. It was a constant struggle to keep the man out of her mind, a struggle that left her weaker with each passing day.

Damn him! The chalk broke against the board, but Savannah kept writing with the stub in her fingers. The giggling behind her increased and the whispers grew louder.

She had hoped that starting school would lessen the tightness in her heart, that keeping busy with classroom work would ease the pain of Jake's rejection. But it hadn't. If anything, the ache in her chest only intensified.

Before she'd met Jake, Savannah had vowed she'd never make a fool of herself over a man. And now she was the biggest fool of them all. She was in love with a man who would never love her back.

She suddenly realized that the room had grown quiet. Suspiciously quiet. From the corner of her eye, she glanced at Emma who sat in the first row, corner seat. She was staring blankly at an open book in front of her. The little girl behind her leaned forward and tapped Emma's shoulder, forcing her to turn around.

Emma's eyes widened. With a frown, Savannah turned. Jake!

Her six-foot-four cowboy, complete with a brand-new black Stetson, blue jeans and denim jacket, stood at the back of the room, arms crossed as he leaned casually against the wall. He grinned at her, then winked at a little red-headed girl who was staring intently at him. The whole class giggled.

Savannah's heart was beating so hard she could feel it in her throat. *This doesn't mean anything,* she told herself. He's just here to see Emma.

She quieted the girls, then straightened her shoulders as she looked at Jake. "Class, this is Mr. Stone, Emma's brother from Texas. It appears he's dropped in to visit with her."

Jake's smile broadened. He pushed away from the wall and walked toward Savannah, every step laden with masculine sensuality and purpose. "Actually, Miss Roberts," he said, "I came to see you."

Her heart lurched and she shifted nervously from one foot to the other. What in the world was he doing? She was in a classroom, for heaven's sake!

Every little girl watched, eyes wide, as Jake moved lazily between the rows of desks to the front of the room.

"Perhaps you'd like to make an appointment to come back after class," she suggested, twisting the stub of chalk in her hands.

"I've wasted enough time as it is," he said, holding her gaze with his. He stopped in front of her. "I'd like an appointment now."

"Jake," she whispered frantically, her gaze darting from the children back to him, "we're having a history lesson."

"You know what I like best about history?" he asked, moving closer to her. "It's not only in the past where it belongs, but it's a great way to learn about mistakes. If you pay attention, you learn a lot from those mistakes."

What was he saying? The chalk suddenly felt damp in her shaking fingers.

"Now if you were having a math lesson, I could show you how the sum of one plus one is greater than two." He stopped in front of her. "Or if you were having a science lesson, I could explain how the diamond is made of pure carbon and is the hardest substance known on earth."

He reached into his pocket and pulled out a small black velvet box. "In fact, I believe I have an example of that process right here."

He opened the box and a brilliant solitaire sparkled from its satin holder.

Savannah gasped. Every child in the room leaned forward, watching with bated breath as Jake took Savannah's hand and slipped the ring on her finger.

She stared at the diamond in disbelief.

"Class dismissed," she whispered hoarsely.

No one moved.

Jake smiled. "Then, if you had a spelling lesson, the first word would be idiot, the second, apology, and the third—" he took her chin in his palm and lifted her face to his "—marry. Used in a sentence it would be, 'I love you. Will you marry me?'"

It was almost impossible to breathe, let alone speak. "But what about you ... what about the ranch?"

He smiled at her. "I leased out half of Stone Creek for the next two years. I'll have to do some shuffling with the herd, but the income not only puts me in the black, I'll have enough to expand."

"Leased out Stone Creek? To whom?"

"To Sam."

"Sam?" Savannah's eyes widened. "You mean you're..."

"I've mended some fences, Savannah," he said softly, "and tore some others down. Shoot," he said with a grin, "his cattle were on my land half the time, anyway."

He pulled her into his arms then, and the silence was so profound you could have heard a feather drop. "Will you marry me, Savannah? Without you in my life, nothing I've done or will do matters to me."

Savannah looked at Emma. Her niece was on the edge of her seat, her blue eyes wide with anticipation. The rest of the class was spellbound as they waited expectantly for Savannah's answer.

She looked back at Jake. He was waiting.

"Yes," she breathed.

The girls clapped and cheered. Jake smiled and lowered his mouth to hers. A collective sigh echoed in the room.

"Tell me you love me," he said, lifting his head.

She smiled slowly and touched his cheek. "I love you, Jake Stone. More than I can ever tell you."

"Then I guess you'll have to show me." He kissed her again, drawing her close to him as he whispered in her ear, "And then, if you were having an anatomy lesson, I could demonstrate what happens when a man kisses the woman he loves and—"

"Class dismissed," Savannah said again, and this time they obeyed.

Emma ran to Jake and Savannah and threw her arms around them. "You're the best big brother in the whole world," she said proudly.

Savannah agreed. She also thought he was going to be the best husband and father in the world.

And as soon as they got back to Stone Creek, she intended to create a legacy of their own.

* * * * *

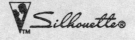

MILLION DOLLAR SWEEPSTAKES (III)

No purchase necessary. To enter, follow the directions published. Method of entry may vary. For eligibility, entries must be received no later than March 31, 1996. No liability is assumed for printing errors, lost, late or misdirected entries. Odds of winning are determined by the number of eligible entries distributed and received. Prizewinners will be determined no later than June 30, 1996.

Sweepstakes open to residents of the U.S. (except Puerto Rico), Canada, Europe and Taiwan who are 18 years of age or older. All applicable laws and regulations apply. Sweepstakes offer void wherever prohibited by law. Values of all prizes are in U.S. currency. This sweepstakes is presented by Torstar Corp., its subsidiaries and affiliates, in conjunction with book, merchandise and/or product offerings. For a copy of the Official Rules governing this sweepstakes offer, send a self-addressed, stamped envelope (WA residents need not affix return postage) to: MILLION DOLLAR SWEEPSTAKES (III) Rules, P.O. Box 4573, Blair, NE 68009, USA.

SWP-S395